Born in the mi   many
years taught En   recently at a Cali-
fornian university. Together with his wife and daughter
he lived abroad for seven years, three of which were
spent in Madrid. He also lived in Japan and Argentina. A
published poet, he is the author of the highly-acclaimed,
bestselling literary novel, SNOW ON THE MOON.
MAN'S LOVING FAMILY is the third in his unusual
trio of crime novels, following the career of George Man,
a parish watchman in eighteenth-century London. Now
retired from university teaching, Keith Heller lives in
California where he writes full time.

Also by Keith Heller

Snow on the Moon
Man's Storm
Man's Illegal Life

Man's Loving Family

Keith Heller

HEADLINE

First published in 1986
by WILLIAM COLLINS & CO

This edition first published in 1998
by HEADLINE BOOK PUBLISHING

First published in paperback in 1999
by HEADLINE BOOK PUBLISHING

10 9 8 7 6 5 4 3 2 1

ISBN 0 7472 5686 1

Printed and bound in Great Britain by
Clays Ltd, St Ives plc

HEADLINE BOOK PUBLISHING
A division of Hodder Headline PLC
338 Euston Road
London NW1 3BH

To my father, my mother and my sister

A chaque assassinat prémédité préside un cérémonial préparatoire et toujours, après, un cérémonial propitiatoire. Le sens de l'un et de l'autre échappe à la conscience de l'assassin.

Jean Genet, *Notre Dame des Fleurs*

This third adventure of the eighteenth-century London watchman, George Man, is a fictionalized re-creation of an actual murder. The times, the places, and the external circumstances all come as near to historical truth as the scant surviving records permit. Surrounding the murder are a number of people who have also been drawn from life. The novelist Henry Fielding is here – engaged in a somewhat surprising occupation – as are his future supporter, the eccentric Bubb Dodington, and the eventual publisher of *Tom Jones*, young Andrew Millar. The deadly Justice Page, the flamboyant John James Heidegger, the all-knowing Ned Ward – each is in his rightful place. The unhappy poet, Richard Savage, is prodded on to centre stage, and even the great Formosan impostor, George Psalmanaazaar, emerges for an act or two from his wretched obscurity in Ironmonger Row. Yet the student of history should not search too minutely through these pages for a perfect factual accuracy. I have tampered freely with the backgrounds and the secondary actions, revised biographies at will, invented whole families and motivations in order to add personalities to the names and complications to the events. The result is fiction – but, I hope, a not completely improbable fiction. History is necessary – it is where we start from – but it is never the same as story. It can tell us what happened, but it can only rarely tell us who.

Keith Heller

Chapter 1

Old Street always looked distinctly different in mid-October. For a week or so, as the autumn deepened into early winter, it seemed to narrow and shorten, the rough stones of the road grew more rounded, the tops of them almost erased. Horses became blurred in passing, and all the people seemed dressed in greys. The air was heavy, a pale brown in colour, and even the texture of the light seemed worn and ancient.

George Man passed between the opposing entrances into Brick and Golden Lanes and continued up the street. It was early evening, but the sky seemed already blacker than it had only a few days before. At one side of the street, a soot-covered man steadied a bowed ladder against a post, while at the top a boy struggled with a flaming torch and cursed the frosted wick. Man had passed on, before the lanthorn finally began to burn and smoke.

He walked slowly, methodically, with the patient steadiness of a middle-aged man who is used to walking. His hands were shoved into the deep pockets of a plain winter coat, as if he were unsure how to carry them when they were empty. His hat hung limp, still saturated from a quick shower that had come at him from a clear sky over Long Lane. He was frowning with worry and not noticing much of what he saw.

The street held too much traffic for a Tuesday. Harried countrymen drove herds of mud-caked cattle and sheep that straggled across the roadway; squads of boys lugged baskets of spilling vegetables; a lace-maker ran past with his merchandise fluttering from his arms, followed by a skinny man with a jingling carton of snuffboxes. They were all headed in the same direction – not towards the City, but towards Westminster. And they were all in the same mad rush.

Even the people of Old Street were more excited than usual. They stood outside talking too loudly, when they should have been tending to their shops. Even the cleanest children were still out at play, taking advantage of their distracted parents. The most respectable tradeswomen swayed giggling from house to house, exchanging news, while the lanky apprentices were drunk at an hour that was too early, even for them.

Man threaded his way through the crowd, ignoring it. He was almost the only one making for the northern edge of the city.

When Man finally neared the turning into Ironmonger Row, he saw a band of four men approaching from the opposite direction. Loud and coarse men, swaggering with the false courage of drink and numbers. Man watched as they elbowed a meek shopkeeper out of their way and flung insults at a lady in a fine coach hurrying past. At any other time, he would have stopped them, demanding to learn their business, and perhaps have herded them towards the nearest watch-house. But today he stood unmoving in the middle of the road, letting them pass by, their long iron swords tapping sharply across the stones; then he moved on into Little Mitchel Street and past the churchyard, quickly forgetting about the rowdy men, as if they were none of his concern.

Ironmonger Row was less crowded, quieter, lonelier. Man's rooms were over a bake-shop, the dimensions of which were extended out into the street by the palpable aroma of day-long cooking. Outlined in the lighted doorway stood the mountainous figure of a woman who was busy scrubbing her hands in her skirts.

'You're come to home early again, Mr Man.' Her voice out of the shadowed face was thick as lard.

Man had one foot on the outside stairway that led up to the first floor, as if this might help to shorten the conversation.

'We're promised a hard-running night, by the first shape of it. And tomorrow's will be the loudest of the year.'

'Aye, then you're best freed of it.' She shook her great head, and a fine mist of flour descended from her hair, catching the light. 'Yet to lose the Mistress as well is now a deep knock on you, Sir. Be there anything at all a body might do for thee – well, my man and me's not so pressed as we can't give another aid. You're not here alone now, I'll have you to know.'

Man hesitated. He slowly scraped the sole of his boot against the edge of the step and finally spoke without looking at the woman.

'There is the rent . . .'

'Which shalt be paid when 'tis paid,' the woman bellowed heartily, 'and not so much as a pinch before!' With a surprising swirl of skirts, she bustled inside and left Man to climb his stairs alone.

The rooms were dark and cold. There was a smell of dust and bad air. Man slid his way carefully across the sitting-room floor, shuffling through scattered or discarded pamphlets and news-papers, to the bitter smell of the fire-place. He worked slowly and meticulously at setting the fire, as if this were the most important task he had to do today.

With the growing fire fitfully lighting the room, he doggedly set about putting the place in order. He knocked his pipes empty into a flat dish, straightened the lap-robe over the back of his favourite chair, replaced a flattened candle. The reading matter on the floor he returned to a shelf in a messy bunch. He scraped a hand across the table for crumbs, then deposited them hastily in his pocket. He picked idly at a plate of broken bread and cheese as he carried it into the kitchen. He had not even glanced towards the spare chair with its compact sewing-box and neatly stacked folds of cloth.

In a few minutes, Man was settled into his chair and busying himself with his pipes. The new candle hissed on a small table beside him and dripped tallow on to the handle of a large pewter tankard of warm ale. It took him almost a full hour to pick away with a penknife at the black cake inside the pipe-bowls and ream the stems with a long twisted straw. It was a weekly chore that usually had him fidgeting nervously to finish, but tonight he seemed to welcome the long tedium of working mindlessly with his hands. Then he filled one of the pipes with the same tiring patience – separating the moist shreds of tobacco, cramming them into the bowl with a lead stopper, checking the flow of air through the stem after each fill. The room was too quiet, and the occasional passing shout from the street only seemed to isolate him more as he bent over his work.

Man tried to read. He sifted through the newspapers – first *The Post Boy* and then *The Flying Post* – but the political hysteria soon wearied him, and he dropped them to the floor. He picked up a book that had been published last year and that he had been trying to finish ever since; but the embittered allegory of reasoning horses still made him suck noisily at his pipe in disgust, and he quickly threw it aside. Finally, he simply rested his tankard in his lap and his pipe upon his chest and sat musing in the half-warmth of the weakening fire.

He did not move, but he could not keep still. He shifted his legs restlessly and tapped his fingers against the side of the empty tankard. He looked into the darkest and emptiest corners of the room, seeing something that was not there, and kept drawing at his pipe even after it held nothing but dead ashes.

When, at ten o'clock, a sudden knocking sounded upon the door, Man jumped eagerly to his feet and hurried across the room, carrying the candle before him. He tore open the door even before he stopped moving.

And then he stood looking at the last person in all of London and Westminster whom he could ever wish to see.

Chapter 2

Man had to serve him something, so he poured him out a shallow cup of the palest wine he had in the house. It came from a bottle which the Widow Manneux had begged him to carry out free from her shop, The Carved Balcony, as a personal favour to her. She knew he hadn't enough money to buy.

Man sank back into his chair and set himself to filling a fresh pipe, tucking the tobacco into the bowl shred by shred. He refused to look towards his guest. The fellow had come knocking at his door at this late hour. Let him begin it.

But George Psalmanaazaar, long-since inured to the coldest of receptions, only sat relaxed in his chair near the fire, one thin and crooked leg scissored over the other, his cup of wine resting easily in his narrow lap. He had turned himself so that the erratic fire could highlight his long curves of fair hair, colour his large oval eyes and powdered skin, accentuate the almost womanish bow of his mouth. The incurable vanity of the man – this appearance of discovering a mirror in every blank wall – was only the simplest of the many things about his peculiar neighbour that so irritated the watchman.

Man had known Psalmanaazaar for something less than a year now, but he had known of him for much longer. There were none in London, and few in England, who had never heard of the notorious Formosan who ate his meat raw and sang eerie songs to the rising and setting sun. During most of the first decade of the century, George Psalmanaazaar had gained as much admiration – and ridicule – as any man in the town.

He had been brought to England from Rotterdam by the Reverend Doctor Innes at the end of 1703, an awkward and awestruck, ragged young man who could speak better Latin than

5

English. The Church had welcomed him loudly as a convert from paganism and as a vocal enemy of the mad Jesuits, while the rich and the important had held him up as one of their most fashionable freaks. Then, in 1704, had appeared Psalmanaazaar's *Historical and Geographical Description of Formosa*, complete with illustrative cuts and translations into the Formosan tongue. This had earned the meek Oriental inflated fame and won for him the patronage of Henry Compton, Bishop of London. For the next four or five years, the reclaimed savage had had the run of the finest parlours and coffee-houses in the city.

Yet even at the height of the Formosan's glory, doubts had begun to multiply. Father Fountenay had scoffed at his Chinese, Dr Halley had undermined his astronomy, the Earl of Pembroke had sworn that no man could learn classical Greek at the University of Formosa. Psalmanaazaar had defended himself as best he could – if his skin was fair, it was due to his having lived in cool underground apartments away from the toasting sun – but the end had come quickly. By the time of Queen Anne's death, the town had mostly tired of the novelty. And by now, opinion was evenly divided between outright mockery and superannuated wonder. The town had agreed upon one thing only – to forget the Formosan and let him settle into poverty and obscurity in a dark pair of rooms only a few houses up the street from Man's.

The watchman himself had been sceptical of Psalmanaazaar's story from the first, yet he had never been able to disbelieve it completely. He had heard tales almost as outlandish as the Formosan's before – and seen them proved true. Besides, if the man's history were nothing but wholesale fabrication – a single monstrous imposture – it would mean that Psalmanaazaar possessed one of the most audacious and fertile imaginations of the age. And that Man would never admit.

He was jealous, of course – always harbouring a secret and yearning curiosity. Perhaps it was Psalmanaazaar's easy intimacy with the great and the powerful that galled and exasperated Man the most. It was a familiarity that he knew he would never have.

But there was something else, too. Had not Man come home exhausted one morning last spring to find Psalmanaazaar in close conversation with Sarah, his hand all but resting upon her knee and Sarah showing all her teeth in a braying, uncontrollable laugh?

A prolonged slurping from the Formosan signalled the end of his wine and of the strained silence in the room.

He looked about him with a sudden frown.

'But we are wanting the good Mistress Man this night, are we not? If I had known she was abroad, I should not have come to intrude myself upon you.'

Man wondered for a moment if he were being teased.

'She is to her father's house.'

'All the night?'

'Yes, all.' More to himself than the other, Man added: 'As if she were needed more there!'

Always the ideal guest, George Psalmanaazaar struck a pose of embarrassed sympathy, his eyes on the floor, and murmured: 'Such is always the woman's refuge – is it not? – when there occurs discord in the marriage.'

Man rapped the bottom of his pipe viciously against the edge of the small table, meaning to settle the tobacco in the bowl, but the top layer of ash sprang out and coated the back of his hand. The Formosan continued to aggravate him. He could have withstood the impertinence of the fellow, but his affected Gallic pronunciation of the word 'discord' was too much.

'If my wife keeps herself away from her home, it is for her mother, Sir, who has been ailing these many months and is now worsening rapidly. The physicians do not give her any promise.'

Man had taken his wife over to Dartmouth Street this afternoon. The house was unnaturally silent. Sarah's father, Michael Wells – stronger than ever at seventy-five – had been moping disconsolately from room to room, an unlit pipe clenched between his teeth. His wife lay in an upstairs bed, looking thinner and more blanched than the sheets, with a pale greyness about the eyes that Man had not been able to look at long. When he had left, Sarah had not seen him to the door.

'A canker, is it?' Psalmanaazaar said it eagerly, but with an undertone of worry, as if he were afraid of catching the disease by speaking of it.

Man grumbled something, stood up, and walked heavily towards the kitchen. This time he brought out the good wine.

'She is aged, I should imagine?' the Formosan went on, holding out his cup.

'Seventy, if an hour.'

The show of pious resignation comes next, thought Man, and he saw it in the slow nodding of the bowed head and heard it in the lengthy sigh.

'We none of us know neither the day nor the hour,' intoned Psalmanaazaar, 'but like the thief in the night . . .'

Man emptied his cup in a single motion and poured himself another. He was in the worst of humours.

'Sir, what is too neatly forgot in these our times is that a man is deliberately designed to be mortal. He grows, he ages, he sickens, and he dies; and there is nothing in that which lies in any way contrary to nature. I can feel the lady's pain, of course, and my wife's; yet the mother has enjoyed a long life, and a good one. Death is not the worst. Many a man is made to bear such pain that may make his own small passing seem a handsome rest.'

Man had spoken out more passionately than he had intended, and now he stared hard towards the darkened kitchen, ignoring Psalmanaazaar's presence.

How could he speak to such a man of a cold day in March, the wind keen and the sky hung with great grey bunches of clouds, and of a huddled group of men and women standing in pairs, all talking at once or weeping or shouting in rage? Or of the ship riding low in the Thames, crowded with small unmoving figures, twenty or thirty or more, all bound for America or the West Indies, hopeless captives of the professional kidnappers called Spiriters who would trade them like livestock to the plantations. The fathers and mothers on the shore aching with helplessness and misery, none of them rich enough to buy their children back.

And among them had stood George and Sarah Man, trying to recognize among the receding silhouettes at the ship's rail the blurred figure of their only son, Nathaniel, aged four.

The sixteenth day of March, 1711. A Friday. He would be a man now . . .

Man looked dully about the room, as if he did not belong here. For the first time in years, he noticed the close smothering smell rising from the bake-shop downstairs.

'At the very least,' Psalmanaazaar was prattling on, 'the good Mistress Man ought not to miss a moment of the festivities tomorrow. 'Tis whispered about that Queen Caroline will be fair drenched in jewels, the greater part of them only lately hired. The event promises to be most magnificent. The Coronation anthems are to be supplied by Mr Handel himself!'

The Formosan's words gradually brought Man back into focus, took his thoughts away from himself. Psalmanaazaar was right, of course; tomorrow would prove to be an unforgettable day for all.

Tomorrow – the eleventh of October, 1727 – England was to have a new King and Queen, and Man wondered if the people were really prepared for it. They had been waiting long enough: since the sudden death of George I last June in Osnabrück, the town had seemed to be holding its breath in barely-controlled anxiety. What would happen when the Prince of Wales was crowned the second German king of England? Some said he was still too young – only forty-three – and still untested. Too many remembered the troubles that had followed upon the death of Queen Anne in 1714, and they gathered together in the streets and in the coffee-houses to compare their worries. And even those who thought the coming of George II to the throne would be calm and easy could not entirely conceal their reservations: the son seemed to be even less English than his father.

The watchman, relaxing a bit, treated himself to another cup and studied his uninvited guest more closely. The Formosan was about as far from being English as any man could get, yet he seemed more excited than a drunken redcoat.

'Do you think the new King will make any great improvement upon the old?' Man asked him.

George Psalmanaazaar first looked at Man with suspicion, then shifted his eyes to the fire and slowly spoke to it.

'It is difficult to say, Sir, difficult. He is a good man, though – full as good as his father was, don't you say so?'

'No, I don't.'

The watchman could hear Psalmanaazaar cringe audibly at the blunt reply.

'We can only hope,' Man went on, enjoying his own nastiness, 'that the second George will find the time to learn a few more words of our speech than did his father. Perhaps such education could keep some more of our poets from starving or from having to sell their shoes for bits of candles. We have fallen far from the days of the late Anne, when a man was not only honoured, but paid for the work of his pen.' Man slyly softened his voice. 'You must know this, Sir, as well as any.'

A muted moan escaped from the Formosan, but nothing else. Man had salted a fresh wound. He had heard that Psalmanaazaar's fortunes had taken a lower turn of late and that he was now wearing himself thin drudging away at whatever dreary work the booksellers stooped to give him. Another Grub Street ghost, and a foreign one at that.

But the Formosan was not beaten. 'I suppose you will have to come earlier than most to Westminster Abbey tomorrow, will you not, Mr Man?' His voice sounded as if it had been oiled.

'I will not come, Sir, neither early nor late.'

'You will not—?' The face swelled into an elongated egg of surprise. 'But you are of the watch, no? And order must be kept. Think of the bullies and canters, Sir, who will be there!'

Now it was Man's turn to squirm, though he used the familiar fumbling with his pipe to try to mask it.

'If you must know, Sir, I have not been employed in the watch for these many months – since June, in fact. My name has not been posted, I have not been looked for, and every constable whom I have treated to a cup of ale or coffee has finally turned me away with an empty promise. What little work I have done of late has been private and has come to me through friends: the watching of a house or a shop, or a night's guarding of a warehouse. But even these – ' Man finished with a troubled sigh – 'even these have come to fail me now.'

There was a long silence. Ironmonger Row, that should have been lifeless by this hour, was still bothered at times by clattering wheels or drunken oaths. Inside the room, the crackling of burning tobacco made a smaller sound.

Craftily, as if he were easing each word through a slot, Psalmanaazaar said: 'And your family's brewing trade . . . ?'

'Sold, Sir, too long past.' Man looked up from the fire. 'But how is it you know of—'

'But this is strange, Sir. Most strange! How has such a sad disorder been allowed to come to pass?' the Formosan asked with the exaggerated shock of one who knows already.

Man grumbled, 'I have none to thank, Sir, but the great Mr John James Heidegger himself!'

'What? He that is to supply the illuminations at the Coronation tomorrow?'

'The same. I hope never to see that fawning toad-eater again in this life!'

This was simply too much for the careful Formosan to digest. A deep, hot bubbling as of trapped gas sounded from the centre of his sparrow's chest.

'But what is the cause of it all, Sir?' Psalmanaazaar squeaked. 'What could have grown this tension between you?'

'I'm sure it is no news to you, Sir,' Man began impatiently, 'that Mr Heidegger enjoys the love of the Court. There is even talk of the new King's making him the next Master of the Revels at a near date. And a finer monkey for the office could not be found between here and Tothill Fields!' Man paused, then went on in a lower tone. 'It was my misfortune to be at my normal work in the Haymarket one night last June. My walking took me past the Opera House at the end of the masquerade – or, as it is so neatly named these times, "ridotto"– one of those midnight gatherings which the Swiss Count sponsors as an excuse for lewdness and promiscuity. I happened to be just without at the discharging of the players, and I caught sight of one made out to be a Mother Shipton whom I knew for a low whore that a warrant had been prayed against. I had only made to lead her off, when her partner set himself betwixt us – a puffed-up man hiding behind an Italian mask. After the fewest words, he drew his hanger against me, and I was forced to level him with my staff. Mr Heidegger was all the while looking on and came panting to the masked gentleman's aid. As it proved, the man was my Lord W——, on whose favour the Count hopes to rely.' Man had been expecting to see Psalmanaazaar wince at the mention of the name, but he was disappointed. 'Since that day, I have not worked, and I have more than once been set upon by hired bullies in narrow lanes. I am old enough and have seen enough to know that merit and intention count for little in this age, so I am not greatly surprised at my fate. But it is still hard, Sir, and I am still without my work.'

What was it that gave Man the impression that he was telling the Formosan nothing new, nothing that Psalmanaazaar did not already know, perhaps better than Man himself? Was it because, after Man had finished, the other did not respond as he should have, with a weary shaking of the head and an indulgent comment upon Man's inability to deal easily with his betters? A cow in a cage, he should have called him, at the very least. Instead, Psalmanaazaar merely sat mute as a stone, his slumped body etched by the colourless fire. He might have been dozing or ruminating, but Man sensed that he was planning something, something carefully thought out in great detail.

Man was thinking, too. He was wondering first what had brought the Formosan to his house. The two men could hardly be called friends, and they had no business or other friends in common. And whatever his jealous fears might be, Man could not really believe him capable of making love to his wife. And he trusted Sarah, simply and without effort.

Then there was the subtle way in which Psalmanaazaar had steered the conversation towards Man's work – or his distressing want of it – as though the Formosan had had the topic in mind all the time. Man had enough to worry about: he and Sarah had been living for nearly a month now upon the kindness of friends and shopkeepers, and Man did not think they could go on much longer. The shadow of the Mint, the hopeless debtors' prison, was nearing their door. What he did not need now was the extra burden of his private troubles being broadcast the length and breadth of Old Street. What he needed was honest, steady work.

Man looked suspiciously at the inert figure of George

Psalmanaazaar, wishing he would go. The fire was waning, the candle was fattening in its sheath of tallow, the room was getting colder. Man did not know the time. Again he caught the aroma of cooking from downstairs, and it made him feel lonelier than ever.

As if he had waited just long enough, Psalmanaazaar suddenly roused himself and crooked his thin body towards Man.

'A man, Sir,' he began cautiously, 'should not be thus separated from his rightful trade, when he has done naught save follow it to the best of his power. Any man has the right to work, if he has none other.' Squirming in his chair, he added quickly: 'You are willing to take, Sir, whatever employment offers?'

Man hesitated, but only for a second. 'Whatever I can do without shame.'

Psalmanaazaar nodded a dozen times, squirmed again, then jumped to his feet.

'We are to talk on it, then. 'Tis why I am here. But first, Sir, the jordan, if you please. Men our age . . .'

Smiling in the dark, Man lent him the candle and directed him to the pot in the bedroom.

Man slowly filled a pipe, politely trying not to listen to the feeble splashing, and turned his thoughts towards what the Formosan might be planning to tell him. It helped him not think too much about how badly he missed Sarah.

Chapter 3

'If I have said much on Mr Abraham Sinclair's great earlier successes in the importing of wines, tobacco, spices and the suchlike, it is only that you may rightly judge of the high turn his fortunes took after the year seventeen-two. He was as close to Sir George Rooke as I am to my breeches; and when that man raided Cadiz and uncovered the barrels of snuff as bounty, Mr Sinclair was waiting with the dockmaster to claim them for his own. Now, as any man knows, there is since that day not a single gentleman who dares show himself abroad without a fully-charged snuffbox in his pocket or in his hand. And it's all of Lombard Street to a splinter of eggshell, Sir, that every second noseful in London's passed at some time or other through the hands of Abraham Sinclair. Most of the tobacco as well, for that matter. Now where do you, Sir, come by yours, as an instance?'

Man glanced at the smoking bowl of his pipe with some embarrassment. 'Oh, this. Well, at whichever of the coffee-houses lies nearest when I run dry.'

George Psalmanaazaar showed his disappointment.

'Yes, well, yet I am sure the better part of it is owed at bottom to Mr Sinclair. He was, I can tell you, during most of Anne's time the principal supplier of Virginia and Spanish to the shop of Mr Benjamin Howes at the corner of Shoe Lane. So many dealers followed his lead that by the year of the Jacobite unrest 'twas said that his signature could be found somewhere within the walls of three-fourths of the shops in the city and every one of them in the walks at the Royal Exchange. I knew him first at that time and heard him once state that, by the aid of a perspective, you could make clear his initials on the skin of almost any coffee-berry in the land!'

15

Mention of coffee made Man yearn for the warmth of a coffee-house and the soothing fragrance of a steaming dish. But he had no money to invite his guest, and there was not a coffee-bean left in the house. Tea, of course, was impossible. The two men were now trying to warm themselves with tepid gin. Outside and in, the temperature was dropping fast and there was a wind.

'How, then, did the gentleman fare during the South Sea tragedy?' asked Man.

'Few better, Sir, few better. He gained something big by it, though to my thought 'twas more due to Mr Walpole's keen eye than his own. The two men have been long close: Mr Sinclair treats the other in the way of being a son, and I dare well say there's none other in England has the face for that – except mayhap for the new King, and he shall be properly tutored soon enough by the Queen Caroline!'

Man was careful not to show in his face any of the disgust he was feeling. It was the Formosan's tone of voice: an oily awe was mixed with a juvenile pride in being able to speak so privately of such great men. Man wondered uneasily if his own voice took on that tone when he spoke of them. He hoped not.

'Is Abraham Sinclair so much older than Mr Walpole?'

'No, Sir; no more than a generation's time. Mr Abraham Sinclair is this year seventy-three. But he has such a strength in him, such a store of native energies, that he commands respect from all who know him.'

'He has a family, I should suppose. An extensive one?'

Here Psalmanaazaar stood up and walked over to the fire to warm his legs.

'If I mean to speak so fully, Sir,' he said with his back to Man, 'of the gentleman's private life, it is with the understanding that none of this is to be advertised to any low news-sheet or runted poet that stands in need of idle tittle-tattle. I have intimated that Mr Sinclair may have some small employment for you, and this obliges you to honour his trust in you – and in me.' He turned around. 'I hope we can be completely agreed upon that score?'

'Completely, Sir,' answered Man, feeling somewhat impatient with the Formosan's gloomy seriousness. He missed the straightforward talk of the streets.

Psalmanaazaar returned to his chair. 'For it is with Mr Sinclair's family, more than with himself, that you are meant to deal – with certain members of it. They have each of them inherited something of their father's spirit – though I have not,' he added wistfully, 'met with all of them myself.'

'Is his wife still living?'

'The present one, yes, that is, his third. She has been with him since the turn of the century. A perfectly sedate woman, she is – some few years younger than her husband.'

Man enjoyed hearing the delicate hesitancy, the never-to-be-uttered disapproval.

'The two previous wives are dead, are they?'

'Oh yes, long since. The second died at the century in her birth-struggles. The first, if I am not greatly mistaken, caught a splinter in her arm in the year 'eighty-three or -four and was carried off at once by an infection.'

The hour was late and the bottle of gin nearly empty, and Man had to work to keep his eyes focused upon the wavering shadow that was George Psalmanaazaar.

'There are some children still surviving, though, I should expect.'

'Of course. There are five of them still, all–all yet living in their father's house.' Once again Man heard the unspoken accent of criticism, and he wondered if Psalmanaazaar were even aware of it. 'Three ladies and two young men. I should imagine that Mr Sinclair must have lost many through childhood sicknesses. He was always, I think, a very prolific man in the begetting of his children.'

'Any natural children, acknowledged or otherwise?'

This was too much for Psalmanaazaar's sense of his own lowered place.

'I could not say, Sir; I really could not say.' He reached nervously for the stone bottle. 'I will repeat what I have said before: Mr Abraham Sinclair is singularly possessed of great animal strengths – especially, I should guess, as regards his secret amours.'

After a respectful silence, Man continued: 'Yet these surviving sons and daughters, I think you have said, are all still living at their first home. Have none of them married, then?'

'No.'

It was the shortest syllable the watchman had ever heard.

Man did not press the point. 'Have the sons followed the father's trade?'

'The elder, yes,' Psalmanaazaar said with quick relief. 'He is in a warehouse at the river. The younger stops still at home, learning from his father the paper of the business. Walter Sinclair is only twenty years of age and is, as I have reason to believe, something less anxious than his brother to steer his life in the course his father has mapped out for him.'

'It is in that young man, then, that some future difficulty lies which moves his father towards employing me?'

'No, no, it is not in him.'

George Psalmanaazaar fell into such a prolonged silence that the watchman had a chance to move over to replenish the fire and warm his stiff hands. The sting of the flames against his cold cheek woke him up a bit. He thought of Sarah, of her dying mother, of his lost work. Now he was more anxious than ever, as he came back to his chair, for Psalmanaazaar to tell him what Abraham Sinclair expected of him.

'Sir, has the gentleman some good work for me, or has he not?' Man raised his voice. 'It may be better that I learn of it from the man himself, if it is his own affair.'

It seemed as if the Formosan stood at the top of a gentle slope and needed only this slight push to send him rambling faster and faster towards the bottom.

'No, no, I must – I will tell you!' Psalmanaazaar's suddenly awakened eagerness gave to his voice a slurred accent that reminded Man of the French silk-weavers in Spitalfields. 'It is this, then. You must know that Mr Abraham Sinclair is not quite like most other men whom you may have known. No, Sir. He is different, he is – himself. These two sons, now, that I have spoken of. Well, they are simply all to him. All! I have never seen, I think, such unmeasurable devotion in a man towards his children. He would do anything to them – I mean to say, to further their name in the city.' The Formosan hacked and swallowed with difficulty. 'Maybe when a man has lost his first—'

'An elder son?' Man broke in, his interest quickening. 'When did he die? How?'

Psalmanaazaar thoughtfully cupped his hands together in his lap. 'To his second wife he gave a pair of twins – Jacob and Sophia – two babes, I've heard it said, as unlike as wine and water. This was in the year seventeen-hundred – early, if I mistake not – but I reckon the year according to the New Style, you understand. Well, I never knew the lad myself, but he was said by all to be a sickly, delicate, dreaming boy with little of his father's driving spirit in him. It must have been a heavy sadness upon Mr Sinclair himself to see his heir apparent bent more towards poesy than towards his father's business.'

'Something outside the father's comprehension, I suppose.'

'Eh? Well, as you say, Sir, as you say,' Psalmanaazaar faltered. 'At all events, the boy died some four or five years ago – was killed, rather, in a way no man pretends to understand. It seems he was standing one day in St James's Park with his intended bride – the two of them in the crowd viewing a display of the Foot Guards – when suddenly a private ran out from the ranks and over to slap the girl full in the face.' The Formosan paused; the watchman abruptly sat forward, tensed. 'What followed then can scarcely be believed, Sir!'

'Perhaps,' Man said eagerly, 'the two men traded a few hot words between them, and the soldier drove the boy into the ground with his musket?'

Psalmanaazaar's whole body jerked. '*Absit omen!* My God, Sir! How–how do you know it so closely?'

'I was there, Sir, though at too great a distance to stop it.' Man waved his magic aside. 'At the end of February, seventeen-twenty-two, wasn't it?'

'Seventeen-twenty-three,' the other said automatically.

'Yes, yes, in the New Style. And the soldier – one William

Hawksworth, I think his name was–was soon enough hanged. What was it, then? Was he jealous after the girl?'

'No, no, none of that. The girl was new to London from Bristol, a daughter of one of Mr Sinclair's keenest competitors. There could never have been any congress between them. Why he chose to slap her, provoking Jacob Sinclair into the affront that ended in his death, is something no man pretends to know.'

'Then Hawksworth must have known Jacob Sinclair and, for some silent reason, harboured a resentment against him.'

But Psalmanaazaar slowly shook his head. 'That, too, is something of a dark enigma, I am afraid. Family and friends all agree that the two young men could never have known each other. The only explanation that has ever offered itself is that William Hawksworth was secretly or for the moment lunatic. There is sure to be much of that malady still in his family. His sister has not been seen outside of Bedlam's walls since his hanging.'

The two men sat without speaking, and the room took its character from their pensive inanimation. Ironmonger Row was by now a boundless emptiness outside the window, and in its depths the roving dog and the huffing sedan-chair appeared and disappeared like the echoes of drops upon a still pond. An unnoticed night-wind slept in the chimney.

Man's thoughts were turning insistently upon the past killing of Jacob Sinclair. He could remember well enough having witnessed it from far off, helpless and unknowing; and now, having been suddenly brought closer to it, he felt that he knew even less than before. Unexplained murder always disturbed his sense of design in men's actions. Violence, he believed, had always its own cause, its own preparation. And the charge of madness brought by others was most often their easy substitute for understanding.

The watchman continued his thoughts aloud. 'If Mr Sinclair should wish me to seek to answer the mystery of his first son's death, I shall try what I can. Yet after such a long period of time . . .'

'No, Sir, no, there is nothing there. That was but an isolated mad act that is best left forgotten in the past.' The Formosan paused. 'I mention it at all only as a first cause of Mr Sinclair's deepening love for his two living sons and of his new dread at their, too, being taken from him. To help him prevent that awful chance, Sir, is the main reason he means to hire you.'

At last he has got to it, Man thought wearily.

'The elder or the younger son? Or the both together?'

'The elder only – now. James Sinclair, he who works for his father at the warehouse by the river.'

'Has something, then, occurred to make him fearful?'

In answer, George Psalmanaazaar reached into a pocket of his limp coat and brought out a much-folded newspaper. He handed it across to Man without a word.

It was a copy of Samuel Buckley's *The Daily Courant*, a paper which Man did not often bother to read for its tiresome Whig fervour. The paper was dated early last week, but its many creases and tears showed that it had passed through dozens of readers. A few light brown stains at the edges told Man that it was probably one of those news-sheets kept at a coffee-house for the convenience of the customers. His eye went to a circled section at the bottom of the page.

ADVERTISEMENT
There is now Publish'd,

The newest annual almanac *Merlinus Liberatus* for the year 1728, containing an exact and useful compilation of all needful and diverting knowledge of events and acts dissipated throughout the coming year. Prepar'd as before by the widely read astrologer and almanac-maker, John Partridge, who did not die the 28th of March, 1708, as reported by some mean wits, nor as rumour'd by many others on the 24th of June, the year 1715, but is now return'd from afar to continue his work. Containing among countless other items a true identification and explanation of the murder of Mr James Sinclair, first son of trader Abraham Sinclair, which happen'd the 20th of November, 1727. Printed for A. Millar at the sign of the Buchanan's Head opposite St Clement's Danes Church.

Reading it over again, Man felt the urge to snort loudly in disbelief. But when he looked up, he saw George Psalmanaazaar trembling violently in every limb, as if he had caught a deadly ague.

Chapter 4

No, he did not like it in the least, waking up alone to an empty house. The bedroom wore a haggard look in the sick light of early morning, and his breath frosting in the thin air made him feel sluggish and old. The other side of the bed seemed hollow, and there was an unnatural quietness from the kitchen that made him suddenly want to call out in anger. Instead, he glowered silently at the bare drab wall opposite the foot of the bed and waited for the grey light to brighten a little before getting up.

Man finally forced himself out of bed, dressed as quickly as he could, and made his way coughing and grumbling towards the kitchen. Before he left the room, he glanced out through the distorting glass of the window at the swelling hurrying in the street below. Scores of them, hundreds, all breathless and talking and laughing, each eager to feel himself a part – if only for a single day – of something bigger. Man grimaced and turned away.

There was little of anything to eat in the kitchen, but Man was satisfied with a draught of small beer and a knob of old bread. A piece of half-bitten hard cheese did not interest him. He had not slept well – again. After thirty-two years of more or less constant work at the parish watch, he found it impossible to get used to sleeping in the dark. Time and again, he would wake in the middle of the night, feeling perfectly rested and ready for work.

Having built just enough fire for one and shunted his chair over to face it, Man sat down to gnaw at his bread and to study again the preposterous advertisement from *The Daily Courant*.

For it was preposterous, ridiculous, not only in its indirect threat against the life of James Sinclair, but also in its assigning the authorship to the long-dead John Partridge. However seriously the threat may have been intended, the reference to the old notorious almanac-maker could only undermine its gravity. Man still felt now what he had felt last night, when George Psalmanaazaar had first handed him the paper: the overwhelming desire to toss it aside and enjoy a long and resounding laugh.

He packed and lit the first pipe of the day, toasting his feet at the steadying fire. Alternating between his beer and his pipe, Man let the newspaper hang limply from his fingers.

John Partridge. A bold-faced charlatan, a low-minded quack, who had enjoyed far more and longer success than he had ever deserved. Man had known him slightly, had seen him in the streets and in the coffee-houses, and he had always marvelled at the unquenchable audacity of the man and the unending gullibility of his customers. The mountebank and his ludicrous prognostications had held the fancy of the mob for more years than Man could remember, at least until Swift – jealous of the astrologer's fame – had predicted Partridge's death in 1708 and followed it with a popular mock elegy. The jest was carried on in *The Tatler*, and Man had joined the town in relishing the almanac-maker's furious efforts to convince everyone that he was still alive.

He was dead now, of course, for good and all. Man was sure of it: he had talked to more than one who had seen John Partridge laid in Mortlake Churchyard. So why now this facetious resurrection of the man and his book? A mere hoax? But including the name of James Sinclair and the specific date made it seem too sinister for a casual display of dark wit. There must be some private reasoning behind it.

Man went slowly to the kitchen for another draught; and when he returned to his chair by the fire, there was no trace of amusement left in his face. The town wits, after all, may have felt nothing but scorn for the pronouncements of John Partridge, but the common citizens had believed in them to a man. They had claimed that he knew more than others, that he had often been seen sailing over the chimneys of Westminster in the company of a known witch. The watchman himself – never normally given to superstition – had sometimes felt that Partridge occasionally came nearer the truth than any man could naturally come. And there were many who said that he was never wrong, only misunderstood . . .

Man shook himself suddenly to drive some warmth back into his limbs. Such thoughts as these could not help him. What he needed to know now was who could have written and submitted the advertisement, and why. Who would want to frighten the Sinclair family so badly that the father should send for a common watchman to protect and defend his son? Whom would it profit to terrify or to kill James Sinclair?

Whoever it was, Man decided after a moment's thought, must not know the family very well. Abraham Sinclair's 'first son' had been murdered more than four years ago – for no reason. Again Man wondered about that. A marching soldier abruptly assaults a girl he does not know and then brutally clubs to death a man he has never met. Could the soldier's family have somehow blamed the Sinclairs and now be planning to avenge his execution? But according to Psalmanaazaar the parents of William Hawksworth had soon after moved away from London – no one knew where – leaving the young sister behind in the deep, inescapable vaults of Bedlam. She was the last child left of the family, and now she was even more finally lost than her brother.

Speculation, thought Man, rising to his feet and briskly stuffing the newspaper amongst some others. Nothing but idle speculation. His work was to watch over James Sinclair and carry him safely past the twentieth of November – nothing more. He should be satisfied with whatever work he could get. He had the Formosan's elaborate letter of introduction which he could present to Abraham Sinclair tomorrow evening, after the distraction of Coronation Day had begun to subside. Presumably, then, Man could also meet the rest of the Sinclair family – the three daughters and the two sons, all still living in their father's house, all as yet unmarried . . .

Jacob Sinclair, Man remembered now, had been about to marry when he was struck down. The girl – the last surviving participant in the drama – was gone home to Bristol, probably married by now. What had she thought, Man wondered, of the prospect of intruding herself into the self-contained society of the Sinclair household? How eagerly had she been welcomed?

The watchman stood still in the middle of the room, thinking; then he looked vaguely about him, trying to decide what to do with himself for the rest of the day.

The streets would be too full for walking. The day's drinking would be hard and continuous, and the young roisterers would not let any man pass in peace. Ladies would be out earlier than usual, offering discounted fees. Everywhere would be the noise and the carelessness of enthusiastic abandon.

An hour later, Man was comfortably settled down with his favourite pipe, a refuelled fire, and a book. The last had not been hard to find: during the past few months, he had had to sell too many of his books and pamphlets to keep scant food on the table. Sarah had often pleaded with him to find some other way, knowing her husband's special love for reading. But there had been no other choice.

Now the watchman was browsing through George Psalmanaazaar's *Description of Formosa*. Man had read it first over twenty years ago, but now to his interest in faraway places was added the intriguing character of the author himself. As much as the Formosan exasperated him, Man could not help being fascinated by the story of his life. Psalmanaazaar had literally travelled the world, experiencing such fantastic adventures as few other men could even hope to dream of.

And his home, the exotic island where he had grown to manhood, was the strangest of all. A place where the hearts of twenty thousand boys were sacrificed each year, where polygamy was the rule and adultery the exception, where the wake for the dead consisted of a merry family feast during which the corpse lay in state upon the table! As Man read on, the London that he knew so well began to seem rather tame and dull to him, and he wondered how Psalmanaazaar could endure his present commonplace existence in Ironmonger Row.

The watchman turned to the fifteenth chapter, 'Concerning their Manners and Customs'. He skimmed through it quickly, until he came to a paragraph near the end.

The first born son of the first wife, as has been already noted, is not to be sacrific'd, and is the heir of the family: Now the right of inheritance consists in this, that he receives one half of the estate after the father's death: But the brethren divide the other half among them; and if every one of them will marry a wife before the death of the father, then the wife whom he marries continues in the husband's family until the father be dead, and then the estate is divided, and each brother takes his share of it, and lives by himself.

There was nothing so very extraordinary about this, but for some reason Man read the paragraph again and again. And when he had finished, he closed the book upon a tuft of ash that had fallen unnoticed between the leaves, as if to mark the place.

'Of course, Sir, I have the book. Of course! Look about you, Sir. Is this not a bookshop? Is this not a place where books are kept and from which sold? Am I not, Sir, a bookman by my inclination, a bookseller by my trade? Yes, yes, I am young and but just now come to it: I am the first to say it. Yes, the shop is small, the books few and helter-skeltered about the floor: I am the first to grant it. But I hope from such humble roots to grow a trade that shall in time bring honour to myself and to my authors. How, Sir, how? I'll tell you, then! I mean to draw the town's attention by printing and offering for sale books and papers that can be found in none other shop. Look here, Sir – and here – and here! Each of these bright and virgin volumes is the work – the newest work, by my faith – of an author who has been dead this past decade at the soonest and whose fleshless fingers can but barely hold the quill. I deal, Sir, in nothing else!'

Andrew Millar was young and thin and quick in his movements – and now steaming in high fury. He stalked as best he could about the cluttered shop as he fumed, keeping always one half-step ahead of his short untidy wig. He kicked angrily at an open tome, gestured contemptuously at a stack of curling pamphlets, and once even spat juicily from one side of the room to the other. His broad forehead shone with sweat, and his rounded chin shivered with emotion.

Man stood calmly out of the young bookseller's path and waited. He knew that Andrew Millar was not angry with him nor with any particular person. His was the wrath of the eager, new tradesman who is left helplessly confused and exasperated before a good opportunity unaccountably missed.

Nervous exhaustion finally slowed the bookseller to a fidgeting prowl. Suppressing a smile, Man asked him: 'You have perhaps been visited by some few other gentlemen seeking the same?'

Young Millar made a wry face. 'You are yourself, Sir, by my latest tally the even thousandth to step in this week in search of the long-mourned Mr Partridge's latest issue. Another few days of this and I shall intend to revive the work with my own hand! Most who come to ask for it – beg for it, demand it – are so soured by my news that I cannot hope to persuade them to any other volume. It is a madness, Sir, and I fear a long harm to my future in the trade. If I cannot supply what I myself am supposed to have advertised, I will not easily regain the city's trust.'

Now Andrew Millar was leaning against a still-empty shelf, his arms folded across his crumpled shirt and his fingers working nervously. Some of his usual good humour had now returned to him, but he was still plainly baffled and worried for his business.

'It was not you, then,' Man said gently, 'that had the advertisement set into *The Daily Courant*?'

'Neither there, Sir, nor in any other of the dozen or so sheets in which it has been shown me.'

The watchman strolled over to a line of books. He scanned the titles and let his hand rest for a moment upon one called *A Journal of a Year of Death*. He smiled grimly to himself.

Andrew Millar spoke up brightly, his sense of business awakened. 'There's more than half a story lies behind the making of that one, Sir!'

'I know.'

Man set the book down and turned back to the bookseller.

'And you have no views yourself to reprint any of the *Merlinus Liberatus*?'

'None, Sir.'

'Would you know if any other printers have such plans?' Man persisted.

Millar's face widened in surprise. 'What man could have? The astrologer's dead these many years now! And the people of these times are something less easily hoodwinked, I think, by such stark foolery.'

'And yet I am hardly the first to come clamouring to you for the book.'

'There is that, yes,' the bookseller admitted.

Andrew Millar was still young and had something still to learn about what the people in the streets wanted and needed.

While the two men stood talking in the shop, a steady current of rattling coaches and discoursing walkers rushed along the Strand and filled the shop's only window, rainbowed with streaks of grime. The hum of the traffic ran through the thick walls of the house as the rumbling of a distant earthquake – only this was constant and unflagging, irresistible.

'If the advertisement be not from your hand, Sir,' Man continued, 'then whose is it? Have you talked at all with any of the gentlemen at the newspapers?'

'Why, we have talked of nothing else together this same week! All agree that they each received it by an extraordinary post – unsigned – but with an important sum of money enclosed.'

'Hardly usual, that,' murmured the watchman.

The bookseller agreed it was a mystery.

'Then who – and why?' Man said slowly.

Andrew Millar felt little uncertainty on this score.

'Well, 'tis a rum jest then, isn't it? By one who means to pretend to the office of the sage Partridge. There's many the like masquerade in print nowadays.'

The watchman was stubborn. 'An expensive joke – and a black one for Mr Abraham Sinclair and his son.'

'I do not know the son at all.' Millar spoke thoughtfully. 'But from what the town says of the father I should expect every third man at the smallest to feel a grudge at him – if not for his exceeding sharpness in his business, then for his brazen fumbling of their wives and daughters. And it may be that 'tis only through the first son that a fear may be settled in the old man that he cannot ignore. I should suppose he favours the young man mightily.'

Man moved idly over towards the window and peered out at the passing crowds. Something that he saw outside seemed to worry or annoy him, and his look darkened; but when he finally turned back to the shop, he was calm and friendly, perhaps even slightly bored.

He came to stand beside the young bookseller and rested his hand upon an unopened crate.

'We can both of us, Sir, invent many reasons to explain the appearance in the notice of Abraham Sinclair's name and that of his son.' Man moved closer and went on in a harder tone. 'But how, Mr Millar, are we to explain the printing in the advertisement of your name, your shop, above any other in the city? Why you, Sir?'

There was no mistaking the insistence in the watchman's manner. The young man straightened up, Man could hear him catch his breath, the bookseller's face looked as if it had just been struck by a slap of cold wind. Involved in his anxiety for his business, he had obviously never thought of it before.

'Well, yes, I can see that now. I hadn't – I mean to say, it had never struck me in that way before. I–I imagine I only supposed my name to have been chosen at the odd chance. There seemed to be no other reason for it, unless . . .' Millar had thought of something. 'There is this, Sir: I had before not expected to open the shop before the next year. My merchandise is far from adequate still. Yet this month I decided to open the trade somewhat early, with a mind to catching some of the Coronation crowds – and even these have mostly failed me,' he added bitterly. 'Perhaps this shop was chosen because 'twas thought to be yet vacant.'

Man nodded his head, but he still looked doubtful. He patted his pockets for his pipe, then realized the shop had no fire and gave it up. From outside came the broken percussion of a raucous band of street-singers.

Andrew Millar stood irresolute and puzzled, and for the first time he looked at the older man with a hint of suspicion.

'Yet you are still quite certain, Mr Millar, that you have yourself at no time met either Abraham Sinclair or his son, James?'

'I have already said as much, Sir.' There was a grain of stiffness in the young man now.

'So you have, Sir, so you have.'

A passing carriage ground its heavy wheel across the doorstep of the shop.

'The nearest I have ever come,' Millar conceded bitterly after an uneasy silence, 'to one of Mr Sinclair's high distinction was in a certain night last summer at Robinson's Coffee-House, when Mr Bubb Dodington demanded satisfaction of me before a crowded room.'

'You had injured him, then?'

The bookseller laughed briefly, but it was not a comfortable laugh and it cost him something to make it. He looked down at the floor and wagged his head, while a shade of pink crept up the sides of his neck and disappeared beneath the fringes of his wig. His fingertips were trembling.

'All unwittingly, I assure you. A man, when he is fairly cup-shot, will often say what he could not defend in the morning. I had been boozing to my shame that night, and I chanced to make some hot remarks against a peculiarly fulsome ditty penned in honour of Mr Walpole's birthday in August of last year. I should not have offered the criticisms had I but known the author, Mr Dodington, was seated at a neighbouring table in company with his stoutest lackeys. If I had not had some few of my own friends beside me as well, I might never have regained the street.'

'You were forced to beg his pardon of him?' Man asked, mercifully not looking towards the young bookseller.

'I would have fought him, Sir, I would!' The voice broke. 'But the gentleman appeared somewhat slow and gouty to me, and his friends better armed than mine. And the offence was hardly meant in earnest. And yet,' he continued with sudden enthusiasm, 'and yet I still cannot find it in me to fault my opinion. The poem is foul, and its manner but another instance of the whoredom of patronage that rules this town. In today's London, Sir, a man must hawk his soul by the hour to feel himself included in the family of the Great!'

Man replied mildly, 'It has been ever such, no better nor no worse.' He looked with sympathy at the young man of business whose single unguarded moment had almost cost him his life and might still dog him far into his future. It was a bad beginning.

'Yet now, Sir,' Millar hurried on, 'a man's thoughts and words are reversed not by the season, but by the minute, by the street. Advantage is all! The vicious man is praised without consideration, the virtuous damned without compunction – all for empty places and preferments. And even these are changed as mindlessly as a lady will change her dress or the patches in her face! Bubb Dodington will sign his name to anything, without regard to its colour or design, and he is these times neither the only nor the worst.'

As if the traffic outside had been listening in, a rhythmic cry of 'Walpole and the King!' passed surging and receding like a long wave down the street. The voices were raw and discordant, almost angry. They picked up other voices on their way.

The watchman shook himself in the chilly room like a great sopping hound.

'I wonder now if two men of such eminence would know each other at all?'

'Who?' Millar asked.

'Mr Dodington and Mr Sinclair.'

'What? Those two? Sir, they're as great together as a pair of loving inkle-weavers! Birds of a single feather, despite the years between them.'

'In the cause of Abraham Sinclair's business, I should think,' suggested Man.

'Oh, now, to be sure.'

'But not at the first?'

The young man frowned secretively. 'Well, now I haven't the whole of the tale myself, but the core of it is this. At some date earlier this year, Abraham Sinclair came to think himself by way of being something short in certain consignments of tobaccos and wines. Nothing, you know, is too small for the eye of that gentleman. He keeps his business as he keeps his house: nothing breathes or moves without his hearing it in his sleep. So the loss was guessed to be either at the warehouse near the river or from the carts during the transport about the town. At a hazard, the old fellow sent for the young thief-catcher that keeps his room in the Little Turnstile just off High Holborn. I cannot mind the man's name at the moment. Do you know him?'

The watchman said he had heard of him. 'Fielding's his name, isn't it?'

'That's it. Henry. A loud and humming canter, by all reports. Just run in from the country, too. Well, 'twas through him that the importer connected with Dodington, for the catcher is rumoured to be one of Bubb's best favourites – what man knows why? Soles his boots for him, I don't doubt, to save the old Jew the ha'penny in the year,' Millar added sourly. 'Whatever the case, this past summer it was that Father Abraham turned the thief-catcher out from his door without a word. I thought myself it would set old Bubb's back up the longest time, but not a bit.'

Man looked idly about him. 'Had he found out the truth, then – the thief-catcher?'

'That's more than I know, Sir. But I can't see Sinclair not knowing the whole of his business, within and without.' The young bookseller sank his voice into a gossip. 'No, Sir. Ask me, and I will tell you it was the youngest girl, Sophia. The catcher probably caught her tail-feathers, and her father wouldn't stand it. What do you think, eh?'

But the watchman was studying an intricate cobweb gleaming dimly in a corner, tracing the maze of its puzzling network.

They were suddenly interrupted by the opening door that let in, with a shaft of random street-noise, the oldest woman in the world. This was one whom age had not merely diminished – it had halved her, creased her over like folded paper. The striated skin of her face had been kneaded into itself like pinched dough. Colourless, almost invisible hairs floated about the head, as if the woman had brought a crown of fog in with her from outside. The whitish eyes were buried within concentric gouges – a single tear would take forever to fall – but the eyes were still as quick and careful as crouching, hidden night-prey.

She wore a Commonwealth coin on a string round her neck, and it knocked against the eggshell bones of her chest as she shuffled with infinite slowness to the centre of the room. She stopped and gazed intently at the stomachs of the two waiting men. She stood low and still as a blasted stump. She had all the time in the world.

Neither man said anything for a time. They felt the embarrassment all men feel when they are confronted with the inexplicably old, the helpless certainty of near-death. And they felt vaguely ashamed of their own comparative youthfulness and strength, the years still left to them.

It was Andrew Millar who finally moved towards her with a gentle smile.

'Is there anything I can help you to this fine day, Mother?'

Nothing living could seem as ancient as her small and wrinkled voice.

'Does the man in the book call in to here any times?'

'What man is that, Mother? Which book? There are books enough in here to keep the both of us busy reading for a lifetime!' the young man said brightly.

'Mr – ' she looked slyly at the two of them – 'Mr Partridge.'

The watchman had begun moving away, but he could still see Andrew Millar's face and its plummeting fall.

'This again, is it? I am sorry to have to grieve you, Madam, but I have to tell you that book is not to be had here at any price or by any caller. The book has not been printed, and it will not be, and none other man in any other shop will say you different. As for Mr Partridge himself – well, Madam, if he stands here beside me now, it is as a spirit from the next world and nothing more!'

The old woman would not be put off. 'I have a something,' she said quietly, relaying an occult message, 'to bring him—'

'Mother! Even this good gentleman here who has been asking so much after it—' and he gestured behind him and turned.

But the good gentleman was gone, and the door was just now closing.

It was three o'clock when Man stepped out of the bookshop and stood at the edge of the churning street. The sky was a dirty grey and cold, but at the level of the street there was a mire of dust and the heat of motion. The stones of the road seemed to be vibrating beneath his feet.

The watchman looked worried. The old woman inside had again put him in mind of the prophecies of the dead quack, John Partridge. The people of London had followed his predictions faithfully for thirty years. Man's own mother had sworn by them. And even now, today, there seemed to be many who still believed in him – at least in the power of his name – as one that could foretell the future without mistake. Perhaps they thought that dying had taught the astrologer even more and that now he knew all . . .

Man looked up and over the heads of the crowds at St Clement's Danes Church across the way. He noticed one figure struggling contrary to the general flow, and he was surprised and suddenly pleased to find him here. Just the fellow the watchman wanted to see.

Man inserted himself bravely into the stream. He had to aim for a spot farther up the street to allow for the power of the current, and he felt as if he were entering a great river in full flood.

Chapter 5

The windows of the bake-shop in Ironmonger Row always wore a fine film of white dust and sweet grease which Alice Kettilby had long ago despaired of ever wiping away. Not that she minded it so much any more: it gave a floury, silvery quality to the light that made the shop seem weightless and restful. It helped to dampen the monotonous thudding of the brake – the nearly century-old kneading machine which Walter Kettilby had inherited from his father – and it diffused the comforting warmth of the shimmering ovens. Even the very air she breathed had the smooth texture of a rich white loaf.

The Kettilbys had come to Ironmonger Row some ten years ago, and their business had prospered. Alice Kettilby was proud of their shop. They made and sold only the finest manchet loaves, and those that were leavened were made with the best ale-barm she could find. Their spice breads and cracknels were loudly appreciated by all, and some of the finer folk came all the way from Westminster for their thick breakfast wigs, the small spiced and sweetened cakes with the delicate sprinkling of caraway seeds.

It was a good shop, selling good wares. There were plenty of bakers in the city – Alice could tell you their names – who whitened their breads with alum or chalk or lead or even with ground bones from the charnel-house! None of that for the Kettilbys. They took their wheat only from those farmers they knew in their home county of Norfolk, and Walter Kettilby ground it all himself with their old hand quern. And if it were a dough that Alice Kettilby wanted to take special care of, she would knead it herself with her own feet through doubled layers of thick sacking. None of her loaves, she swore, could ever be said to have come close or sad, and the Assize would never be dragging her man off for a stand in the pillory for selling underweight breads.

Alice Kettilby was a substantial woman of an indeterminable age, warm and wholesome and yielding as a fresh steaming slice. She was capable and shrewd in trade, but – since the early deaths of all her children – she was inclined to mothering whichever hapless adult lay to hand. Her husband, Walter Kettilby, was a small emaciated man whose body seemed to be composed of little more than projecting bone and unsifted flour. He spoke very seldom, but he twitched constantly. The modest quantities of loaf sugar which the shop dealt in had cost him most of his teeth; and when he had to sample a crisp biscuit, he was forced to stretch his mouth nearly to one ear to centre the bread over his last sound molar. Between him and his wife was the natural bond between two people who work together at a trade they both enjoy and respect. They were a pair.

Today, however, Alice Kettilby was bluntly disappointed. The coming Coronation was not bringing in the eager droves she had envisioned during the past week. Perhaps the people were simply too excited to eat or the shop itself lay too far off the main thoroughfare. Her neighbours in Ironmonger Row had not failed her, but they could not take up all the extra wigs and manchet loaves. She did not like to think of how many would have to be let run stale.

All morning she had been plying worriedly from oven to window and back, as if her needless bustling about could impart some activity to the too-empty shop. She had rubbed out five or six holes in the glass and had stood squinting out at the dizzying crowds in the street. And it was through one of these circles that she had first caught sight of the Bastard.

It was what she always called him. She had heard his name, had even remembered it; but if the man himself were so constantly bent upon advertising his illegitimacy in every lane and alley, then so be it. Some believed him, some didn't; though Alice Kettilby could tell them the truth of it, if they had only thought to ask. She had got it from one who *knew*!

'Well, and what d'you think then, Alice? You didn't think really that one like him was got between the lawful sheets, did you?

Why, you've only to look at him once to see!'

Alice looked at him through the dusted window. A midsized man of thirty or more, thin as a blade, a long horse's face that was hard and coarse, but with the hardness and coarseness of character. It would not be handsome to women, but it might suggest something interesting. If he often carried himself too gravely, it was a melancholy that could soften into an attractive easiness – but sometimes too much so, to Alice's way of thinking. No man need display himself quite so low and common as the Bastard liked to do.

'No, no, no. It was the lady herself that started it all. Don't you remember? The year was 'ninety-seven – the lady, Anne Mason, was still Countess to that fine Earl of Macclesfield, of course – when she began to find herself something swollen in the belly. Well! And didn't she want to give the Earl her last goodbye since the day she wed him? So what does she do, the wise dolly? Why, only tells him the child's not his, but a memory of her short dance between the sheets with the Earl Rivers! And did it answer? Sure as a gun, it did. Macclesfield runs off for his divorce, the Lady races across town to the bed and name of Colonel Brett, and the babe was born a bastard, lucky caul on his face or no. Oh, he's got the blood, of course; but I'd want to see him send his noble blood to market, Alice, and see what it would buy!'

It was almost three now, and the Bastard had been prowling about in the street since just past twelve. Alice Kettilby frowned critically at his motley dress: broken shoes and haggard stockings, loose breeches and limp coat, a slouching beaver on his head, and on his shoulders a cloak that should still have been a deep scarlet in colour and trimmed with costly lace – but it wasn't. The kind of fellow she overlooked in the street every day. But the fine sword that hung at his side worried her – where could he have stolen that from? – and she didn't care for the swagger he affected as he stalked up and down Ironmonger Row, clearly thundering curses at the empty air. She was sure he could never be trusted. She only wished George and Sarah Man agreed with her.

The Bastard had come to see the watchman, of course, she knew that. She had heard someone hurriedly mounting the outside stairs, and then she had seen him coming back down more slowly with a scar of disappointment on his face. He would never think to ask at the bake-shop about the Kettilbys' lodgers: no, he had tried that once. Then she had watched with a shaking head as he had taken up his stand in the street. She could never understand why the Mans loved the Bastard so – it didn't seem right to her, or safe – though she knew he needed every friend he could find.

'Hate him? Of a surety his mother hates him! She pleads her belly to leave her husband behind; and then when the child's a man, he comes round to her door and shouts to be let into her best rooms. Better to keep it all forgot – she's no more use for him – and maybe Colonel Brett, he doesn't like to be minded of the trail his wife's left behind her. You learn from Molly Pheasant, Alice: that lady'll do anything to forget her yesterdays!'

And there was another thing that bothered her, the way the watchman and the Bastard seemed to talk the same kind of language. They both knew the darkest and dirtiest corners of the city and felt at home with what they found there. Theirs was a knowledge of a whole substratum of the population that confused and alarmed her. The harsh-voiced bullies, the crippled pick-pockets, the nasty wet-mouthed women – all seemed to be part of a strange and savage, far-away world. Even that nice Mr George Psalmanaazaar – who some said came all the way from China and once stepped into the shop to eat a handful of uprisen dough – even he did not frighten her half so much as these derelict citizens of the streets. Yet to George Man they were like family!

Just as Alice Kettilby was about to turn away from the window and hurry back to the ovens, something happened out in the street that kept her flour-smudged face pressed against the glass. The tide of activity in Ironmonger Row had begun to diminish, the knots of Coronation spectators had all passed by. Yet the man whom the baker-woman called the Bastard still loitered in front of the house, still scanning both ends of the road and wearing a path in the stones. He looked to her more worried than usual, this time even more desperate.

She wondered at this. If he had come only for some food and a roof for the night, he should by now have given it over and gone to look elsewhere. He must have another, more urgent reason for wanting to find the watchman.

Now she saw him stare more fixedly towards the bottom end of the street and then make a reluctant gesture of greeting. In a few minutes another man came up to join him. This one was smaller and stocky in build, with a permanently reddened face and a glazed stare. He stood in the wincing crouch common to all street-porters, and the woman at the window thought his legs looked even more baker-kneed than her husband's.

The two men moved over to the opposite side of the road to talk. They immediately fell to arguing, that was plain enough to Alice Kettilby. The Bastard was bending over and shouting down into the face of the other man, his lean jaw snapping angrily. The new man was trying his best to answer and calm his friend; but the habit he had of ducking his head as he spoke, as if to ward off a blow over the eye, made him seem cowardly and defenceless. Once or twice the Bastard turned and swept an arm towards the upstairs rooms of the watchman, and then his rough face looked swollen with a dark fury.

It was this that had always disturbed the baker-woman most about Man's friend: this potential she saw in him for sudden, unreasoning savagery. He was a man, she thought, who might be angered into any kind of outrage in a moment. Because he was always so conscious of his own hurts, his own unhappiness, he seemed always ready to strike out at anyone and for any cause. Such men frightened her.

And now in the emptying street the Bastard was looming over the smaller man, and the woman at the window could hear the thick grating of his voice, though not the words. And she saw his right hand swinging reflexively round to the sword at his side and his entire body tightening like a muscle and the other man stepping quickly back and raising his bare hands before him . . .

'Mr Kettilby! Come quick, husband! Come to see!'

Alice Kettilby had to run to the back of the shop to make her busy husband hear. She was gone from the window for less than a minute. But when the two of them returned to peer through the dusted glass, the only man in the street was a disconsolate-looking pieman, carrying an overflowing tray.

George Man sat at one side of a loaded table in a cook's-shop in Hanging Sword Alley, Water Lane. In front of him lay plates of grey peas and bullock's liver and two heavy tankards of porter's ale. The scant remains of pickled oysters, congealed in cold grease, had been pushed aside.

At the other side of the table sat a long, well-built young man with impenetrably curly black hair and the frank look of the country before it is shaded over by the close city streets. He had the healthy vigour of someone who works in the open air by day and at night sleeps deeply and without dreams.

James Gregory was a street-porter by his trade, one who would cheerfully shoulder the greatest burdens without showing the smallest crease in his huge face. Yet now, as he talked to the watchman, he wore the same fuddled look as when he was trying to mouth out a long word in the newspaper.

'Your man Savage may be all you say he is, George,' the porter said gravely, 'but I think I know Bill Merchant about as good as I know my own hand here. And I tell you, I'm damned worried for the both of them.'

For James Gregory worrying was like thinking, something that had to be done more with the body than the mind. Now he bent over his tankard, a clothed mass of knotted muscle, and seemed to twist himself internally like a wetted rope. The watchman imagined he could actually hear something creaking.

The cook's-shop was all but empty: an ancient soldier snoring at the fire, a labourer and his wife wordlessly gumming their beef, their two boys playing at chuck-farthing in a corner. The night was coming on early outside. There would be crackling frost and cold stars.

Man gurgled on his pipe and looked at the street-porter he had known for over two years. It disturbed him to see the young countryman with the dazed, lost frown of a child who has been struck by a friend for no reason.

'It's hard for me to know what to say, Jim. I don't know your

Bill Merchant, you see, not from Adam. What sort of a fellow would you call him?'

'No, Bill's a good enough one – really! – though there's some of the other porters would tell you I lie. But he wears his knot as straight as any of us, though I'll give you he'll be the first to call out the loudest for the lightest load. Yet there's no great sin in that, is there?'

'Is he a hard man?'

Gregory thought this over with his thickened knuckles.

'Well – now Bill took me up, you know, and taught me the carrying, when I first come to the city. And I'll always be much beholden to him for that. Now that's clear.' The street-porter hesitated, then smiled weakly. 'But it is true now that Bill's sometimes more feathers than fight, and he'll let himself talk a little louder than he's got the voice for. You know the kind, George. A dozen of drink and a frown and he'll show you his sword, but another pint and a good word and you won't see it again for the rest of the night. It comes from him being somewhat smaller than most, I'd say. He's always daring more than he's doing, but that don't make him a whole bad man now, does it? Not to my think-ing, it don't. I've seen him too many times with his hands wet as morning grass, though I never let him know I saw.'

The cook's-shop had the full quiet of a home. Man grunted his chair back from the table to make room for his crossed legs turned to the side – an annoying habit that never failed to leave a plateful of crumbs in his lap and his wife fuming.

'How long have Merchant and Savage known each other?' Man asked after a time.

'Not long, I think. As Bill tells it, they first met when Savage needed a man to carry his books over to where the Richmond coach stops. A few bottles of wine later and they were fast friends.' The porter suddenly smirked in prim disapproval. 'There's that about Bill, too, you know. He's maybe seen the insides of too damned many tippling-kens in this city.'

The watchman recognized this streak of country innocence in his young friend. James Gregory was the kind who would do his drinking at the side of a busy street, thirstily tilting back a leathern

43

bottle of ale during his midday rest, a knob of hard bread lying at his feet. He was also, as far as Man knew, one of the very few men in London who never smoked.

Man tried gently to probe at the source of the street-porter's uneasiness. 'Your friend could, I think, choose far worse men for a companion. Dick Savage is a weak man – I'd be the first to grant it – and he often feels his own pain too much more than the pain he sometimes gives to others. He loves himself to excess – and hates himself to his own hurt. I don't know. Perhaps when any man is driven to call himself a bastard all his life – when he fancies a perfect happiness that should be his and isn't – when he thinks himself robbed of his family, of his past—' The watchman let the end of the sentence go in a spurt of uncertain smoke. 'Well . . . But what I mean to say, Jim, is that the man is more to be pitied than feared. He has never been a vicious man, only confused and hopeless. I can't see how he could ever involve your friend Merchant in anything that would bring them to a deep trouble. Savage is simply not that bold a man.'

The two men sat silent, neither looked directly at the other. The sound of the boys at play marked a lazy time through the stuffy shop with a muted ringing and giggling.

Gregory slowly passed the flat of his gnarled hand over his head and down to his neck to work away at the stiffness there that plagued all street-porters.

'That's fine then, George, that's fine. But there's something more in this that maybe you don't know about, something that I'm afraid might bring my best man to a short dancing at the Tyburn Fair. And I can't, you know, just sit and watch that run loose right past me. I can't.'

'What is it, then?'

'Well, there's the knot in it I can't untie. I just don't know enough of it. But I do know there's another man joined with them now, and maybe it's that that's got me worried so.'

'Who is it?' Man asked, more interested.

'Do you know a fellow named Bellamy?'

'I know one called Edward Bellamy who's a housebreaker up in Seven Dials. Is that the one?'

'Well, I can't say. I've never met him yet. He's Bill's mate, you know, and Bill says he's got the lightest pair of hands north of the river.' The street-porter gazed thoughtfully at the backs of his own iron hands. 'Is he dangerous?'

'No, no, not Ned Bellamy. There is not quite enough of him to make a dangerous man. His only failing is that he never knows just when to stop. Even once plundered the house of the woman near Leicester Fields who received for him, as I heard it.' Man tried to urge his slow friend on. 'But what is it, Jim? What's the game?'

But James Gregory needed time to work out an answer. The belching labourer and his wife had finally managed to coax their boys home and to bed and the grumpy proprietor had succeeded in steering the sleep-drunk soldier out of the door, by the time the street-porter had his weighty thoughts in order.

'Here it is, then,' he began ponderously. 'It seems that Bill's got himself all excited to sell something to Mr Savage – something that your friend is hot to get at, that he says is his by his birthright – though what it might be I've no more notion than an African has of snow.'

'Is it maybe something Bellamy has stolen and is holding and your friend Merchant means to handle the trading between them?'

'Why, that's what Bill himself wanted me to think, I do believe. But then why,' he went on peevishly, 'why does he warn me to say nothing of it to the housebreaker himself, if I should ever come up against him in the street? And why does he worry me so to get a clean sheet of old paper, the good vellum that the lawyers like to use? Where's the sense in that, George – you tell me!'

Man had nothing to say to this, but he waved a hand casually. 'Yet even if he wants to pass on some stolen goods, the risk lies mainly, I think, with Bellamy and Savage.'

'I hope so, George, I hope so.' The porter up-ended his tankard. 'But I can't stop asking myself why Bill should so suddenly be in such a running need for money.'

The watchman's snort earned a critical glance from the impatient proprietor.

'Which of us is not, Jim, with the prices in London these times?'

'But listen. This time last week Bill and me were carrying together over in Southwark, and after it was done we stopped ourselves for a pair or more of glasses. I was teasing him, you see, about how flush in the fob he'd be with the money he'd promised himself from Mr Savage. He laughed a bit with me at first, but then he goes all glum in the face and says that the coin will count for naught if he can't get Bellamy to do the deed for him. And when I ask him what it is, he makes as if he doesn't hear me, only groaning and shaking his nob and saying that if it ain't done he's a dead man cold and buried. After that, I can't get anything from him but talk about what place lies farthest from London, as if he'd already got a seat for himself on the next coach.'

'Creditors, maybe,' Man reassured him. 'Nothing more.'

James Gregory grabbed the table and said harshly: 'Then why is he so goddamned scared, George? Why? He's as feared as a man that finds he's been sleeping with a dead woman the whole night! So scared I could smell it coming out of him like bad ale!'

Man saw the great hands of the porter begin to tremble. And he suddenly remembered a morning in his own boyhood – the morning of his first scheduled scrap with the neighbourhood bully – and how his father's hands had shaken, spilling the dish of coffee, and the low, loving voice telling him that he must finish it on his own and to try to be brave . . .

Exasperated into action, the proprietor started to clear the table, explaining to the gentlemen that his wife was waiting upstairs and that she had a tongue on her *this* long. He might have saved his breath. Neither of the men heard a word he said.

Chapter 6

Early in the evening of the next day, Man stood outside No. 2 Soho Square with George Psalmanaazaar's letter of introduction in his hand and suffered. He felt a stranger in this rich air. He saw suits of clothes whose textures his fingers could barely recognize. Accents refined to a chilly brittleness tinkled through the square. The men, even the lowliest, looked through him; the women, not at all.

It had been a trying day for Man. He had risen early, drunk his breakfast, and gone out into streets that were loud with exclamations of wonder and childish delight at yesterday's Coronation. Old men recalled dramas of the past with toothless scorn, staid ladies crooned shrilly of the new King's figure, little girls gawked blindly behind their mother's skirts, pretending to be still dazzled by the Queen's jewels and the array of lights. Man seemed to be about the only one in London to have missed it, but he comforted himself by grumbling that he never cared much for raree-shows anyway.

He had bolted out of the house with his head bowed to avoid the solicitous curiosity of Alice Kettilby and hurried down the waking street. He was heading for Westminster and the home of Michael Wells in Dartmouth Street. Man's father-in-law, now in his seventies, was still one of the busiest and most highly regarded sign-painters in the city, a man who thought that the practical necessity of his trade was no excuse for not putting his best efforts into it. The watchman had always got on well with him: he admired his unflagging diligence as much as his natural skills. Now the old painter was also working at designing trade cards, foreseeing the day when the dangerous projecting signboards would be outlawed from the city's streets.

King Street, Westminster, was a shambles. Man had had to

slog through sodden mounds of refuse, knee-deep in places, and thread his way through sleepy workmen and elated pickpockets. A dozen times he had been approached by men selling fresh slivers of wood which had been accidentally touched by the King or Queen and were now supposed to be able to cure numerous diseases. He had finally had to walk with his collar opened to show the amulet he carried from his childhood, when he had been cured of the 'King's Evil' by the touch of Charles II.

Before going on to the Wells's house, the watchman had turned into the quieter haven of George Yard. Whenever he was in Westminster early, Man liked to share a morning draught with a long-time friend of his who lived in an ageless house cringing between an aromatic chandler's and a dilapidated barber's. And this morning Man had a more urgent reason for stopping in to see his friend.

Homer Wolfe knew more about the printed word than anybody else in London. His single room was an airless repository of every tract, news-sheet, pamphlet, journal or book printed in the last half-century. He neither worked nor played nor bothered himself with anything beyond his front door. He read, as other people breathe and sleep.

He also knew more about diseases, especially his own, than any man alive. And Man had found him with his nose dripping into a thick medical volume and feverishly examining a different part of his wasting body at every new page. He had never been really sick, of course; even now, almost sixty, he was the healthiest chronically ill man the watchman had ever known.

Man had brought back a couple of restorative draughts from the chandler's shop next door: a bowlful of cock ale for Homer Wolfe – they sold the real article there, brewed with a fighting cock in the vat – and a mixture of wormwood in wine, a 'purl-royal', for himself. The two men had sat for a long while over their drinks, the conversation turning almost exclusively upon digestion and skin eruptions with a short digression into the proper contours of the gums.

It was the advertisement of John Partridge's almanac that Man had come to talk about. It still bothered him. Either it was a meaningless hoax, or it was a cleverly disguised warning, deadly serious. Man wanted to know which.

'After all, Mr Man, if it is not a legitimate announcement – and it cannot be that, I should have heard – then it must be nothing less than a direct assault upon Abraham Sinclair and his close-kept brood. Who would bother playing such a humourless jest upon another for all to see?'

'He has enemies?'

'He has friends,' Homer Wolfe had intoned mysteriously. 'And when a man has such friends in such places, he naturally casts a long shadow which cannot help but blacken others.'

A fingertip wiggled violently in an ear, to be followed by a long and doleful inspection of the sample.

'Then why take aim at the elder son, James?' Man had asked.

'The weakest commissure in the Sinclair structure, my friend. The fraying link!'

'How do you mean?'

'Well, he's made himself first cock of the river warehouse, hasn't he? And 'tis his thumb that's at the deepest pulse of the business, not the father's.'

'And that makes him all the weaker?'

'In the family, aye.' And Homer Wolfe had looked at the watchman slyly, unconsciously palpating the glands in his neck. 'For the boy's coming marriage will give him something else to think about than only wines and tobaccos.'

'He is to marry? Do you know the girl?'

'The family, yes. The father is Edmund Windbush, a distiller of good note. The daughter's name is Patricia. A pretty enough girl, I'm told, though her family is somewhat lower than Abraham Sinclair had wished for.'

'When will they marry?'

'Why, somewhere towards the end of this next month, if I remember right. If all goes as planned . . .'

Homer Wolfe had hiked up his nightdress and bent over to compare the dimensions of his calves in order to decide which of them might be inflamed. He had not seen the suddenly blank look on the watchman's face, and Man had not seen the look on his.

As Man had made ready to leave, a costumed servant noisily burst into the room without knocking. His scent preceded him.

'Mr Wolfe, Sir! You are to come at once! Mr Wol—'

An intangible door had slammed shut in his face, and he and Man had bowed coolly at one another.

And that had been only the beginning of the day.

He was to spend the next eight hours in the fine home of Michael Wells, immersed in a choking atmosphere of love and unhappiness and real disease. Hester Wells lay in her bed upstairs, incorporeal beneath strata of covers, not knowing who she was. Servants slumping without energy about the house.

Sarah Man was still determined to stay by her mother's side until the end, and Man had let his own assorted miseries get the better of him.

'Your home, Madam, is in Ironmonger Row!'

The old signpainter had wandered aimlessly down the silent hallways, speechless, grinding the stem of an empty pipe between his teeth, a great hulking figure heavy with pain. At times raising his permanently discoloured hands to his face, as if wondering how they came to be stuck at the ends of his arms. The dulling orbits of Michael Wells and the watchman had sometimes crossed, and Man had had to stop to avoid a collision.

In the middle of the afternoon, a tension had developed in the house that had charged the air. Sarah had wanted her father to let her write to his son, Daniel, informing him of the mother's deepening illness. Man had agreed.

It had brought the signpainter scrambling angrily out of his lethargy.

'I have no son!'

This dated, Man knew, to a time twenty years past, when Daniel Wells had abruptly married a Scottish woman who was staying with relations in London. Then in 1710 he had moved with her to Edinburgh to take up a position in her father's woollen manufacture. The son had never been back since, and the father had never allowed his name to be spoken in the house. There was no room in the family, the old signpainter grumbled daily, for a Scot.

Sarah Man had won out in the end, but only because she had

finally admitted having written to her brother yesterday.

The watchman could still see the effect of it on the father. The pipe had drooped and almost fallen, the red-streaked eyes had glazed over, you had to listen hard to hear the old man breathe. It was a dark colour that had finally appeared in the mix.

'She is dying, then.'

The deadened echo of those words still sounded round Man now, as he stood cold and strengthless in Soho Square. The words seemed to shudder about the open area, imprisoned by the stone faces of the handsome houses, until they were put down once and for all by the noise of clattering wheels, anxious servitude, stern commands repeated.

He had to lean far back to look up at Abraham Sinclair's rich house. It was the third north of the entrance into Carlisle Street on the west side of the square. As it loomed above him – three broad storeys of symmetrical windows crowned by a pair of sharply angled dormer windows and a long black thumb of a chimney – Man felt the vertiginous sensation of being confronted with a heart-breaking slope that he could climb only on his hands and knees.

Not far wrong there, he thought bitterly, as he moved forward to brave the door.

It took just enough time for the watchman to start a sweat in the cold night air to bring a stiffened man who looked frostily at him out of a face like a wedge of porous cheese.

'Good evening. I am here to see Mr Abraham Sinclair, if he could give me a moment.'

It could have been the wind that fluttered the letter in his hand, but there was no wind here at the door.

Man guessed the servant was Irish, with a native aversion to leaving any door open unnecessarily.

A sudden thirst struck the watchman, a bone-searing dryness, but it was too late now. Even if he had the time for a quick cup, he would not know where to go to find it. He did not know this square well. And he might not even know the right words to use in asking for it.

He stood looking at the whole of the darkened square. Within the larger quadrangle of standing houses lay another of grass and walks and a fountain, all enclosed by the gaunt and spiked repetitions of an iron fence. Also inside, he knew, were a few geometrically planted trees, a balanced configuration of statuary, an even number of perfectly tended plots of turf – four more squares within the square within the Square. There could be something very satisfying and reassuring about such symmetrical reasonableness, but for some reason Man found it drab and stultifying. He knew they had such ideal blocks of space inside the prisons, too.

It could be a pleasant enough place by day, of course – a place for the children to run uncensored, for the cooks and maids to compare their employers, for the ladies to be seen and for the gentlemen to see them. As with any of the better squares in London, this one would provide a calming sanctuary from the loudly moving streets that threaded the city together.

But standing here now in the wind, the watchman could not see it – and he suddenly felt a little sorry for himself. So many years on the night-watch. He knew so very little of the day; he was too well-acquainted with the night. To him, Soho Square was only another place that was too dark, too quiet, somewhere a man would run to if he were afraid of being found out.

It was a fact that many of these grand houses were taken by some only to be rented out to another. And often the owners were none too careful about assigning the right names to the right places. A man could lose himself for years in here, lose his past; or he could make sure another man would stay lost for ever.

A quick inrush of icy air was the only signal that the door had been opened behind him.

'Sir?'

With an inward reluctance that he hoped did not show in his walk, Man followed the bloodless servant into the house.

To the watchman, it already seemed to be getting harder to catch his breath.

Chapter 7

Abraham Sinclair was reading Psalmanaazaar's letter of introduction, when the doorman showed Man into the room. The old importer did not look up, but continued studying the lines of close, slanted script. In the time that he made the watchman wait, he could easily have memorized it.

It was cold in the room with no fire. Man missed his coat which had been stripped off him in the front hall with all the polished dexterity of a veteran cloak-twitcher. More than anything else he missed his pipe, but he was not sure if he would have had the courage to smoke it in this room anyway.

It was an almost square room, not a very large one. Its only ventilation would have come from the single window which could not have been unbolted yet this year. Dark greys and dark greens dominated the walls, unrelieved by a scattering of badly hung paintings – unsigned sea battles in unadorned frames. The ceiling was high, but plain. The floor was covered with a featureless carpet, the three or four elbow-chairs with drab and unbrushed material. Of the handful of figures ranged upon the veined mantelpiece, Man recognized a tortured Hercules writhing in his poisoned shirt and a stricken Deianira cowering in fear and guilt.

For whatever purpose the room had originally been intended, it was clear that it was now used for business. A plain table stood to one side of the window, its surface covered with a few stacked books, sheaves of cheap paper, a series of ledgers marked from A to K. Man had never doubted George Psalmanaazaar's glowing assessment of Sinclair's dealings, but now he had some trouble understanding how such successful trading could be carried out in this small room. It was wholly impersonal, frigid, lacking in energy.

But the watchman understood better when Abraham Sinclair finally raised his head from the paper. It was as if the mere act of lifting his face to another man had started in the importer a just-tapped current of power that seemed to surge upward from the base of his spine. The undeniable reserves of animal vitality were always there, as they lay in Man's young friend, James Gregory; but in Abraham Sinclair they were perfectly harnessed and controlled, meted out only in the most exact doses of irresistible strength. There would be no waste.

The man was old, there could be no mistaking that. He wore his own hair, pure white, cropped closely to the flattened skull. The skin of the face was scored with balanced wrinkles and had the granular texture that comes with deep ageing. The projecting ears were tufted, and the eyebrows bristled with greying unclipped hairs, forming an overgrown ridge above the eyes.

And it was the eyes that attracted Man the most – and repelled him. They were the darkest he had ever seen in a man, truly black. The distended irises could hardly be distinguished from the holes of the pupils. Even the whites were shaded and murky. The eyes belonged not to a man, but to some rapacious night-bird or to a stealthy hunting animal that keeps itself close to the ground.

The watchman was staring at a wall-clock framed by a pair of short sputtering candles, when Abraham Sinclair finally decided to speak.

'You are Mr George Man.'

The old voice was strong; it would not readily accommodate itself to questions.

'I am, Sir.'

'Your age?'

'Forty-eight this past July.'

'I like to know a man's age when I trade with him. It tells me most of what I want to know. The young know less than nothing, of course; and the old forget, or they busy themselves uselessly with their dying.' The wells of the eyes probed him. 'You look to be about fit enough for it, for what I have in hand for you.'

'I hope I am, Sir.'

What was wrong with Man? He had met some of the rich

before, the powerful. He had seen a few of them as they really were – poor in spirit, weak, uncertain. What was it about this old man that made him feel younger than he was, less able?

The eyes, of course. They were insupportable in their gross intensity. No matter how large or spacious the room, a man could never hide from them for long.

But there was something more. Abraham Sinclair was the living distillation of his years, of his experiences. He had known every type of man, had himself tried and endured every passion and loss. He had nothing more to learn.

'We'll smoke together.'

Man was about to say that he had left his pipe in his coat pocket, when the importer worked himself to his feet and shambled over to the desk. He brought back two pipes already filled with a coarse, black tobacco. He took a light from a wall-candle with a twist of paper, then handed it to Man.

'A man that does not smoke is not a man,' Sinclair pronounced. 'My steward will bring in the drink directly.'

'Thank you, Sir.'

Abraham Sinclair made the kind of sounds all old men make sitting down.

'Now about yourself.'

For the next ten minutes, the watchman supplied a bare outline of his past career with the watch in the various wards of the city, together with a briefer mention of some of the private work he had done. Yet he said little, gave nothing, of himself. He did not care to show himself too much to the old trader, and Sinclair anyway made no great efforts to listen. These were all mere formalities.

Man finished his recitation just as the steward brought in a well-turned glass bottle and two deep cups.

'You'll like this, Mr Man.' It was an order. 'Right old Irish usquebaugh. I have a puncheon of it shipped me direct every month. A man wants his nipperkin on the hour.'

The two men drank. The liquor was grainy and thick, with the heavy smoothness of oiled water. Man could feel it begin working on him at once.

The importer cracked his neck, smacked at his pipe, wetted his lips – the self-satisfied man's preparations for a long, impressive speech.

'Now because, Mr Man, you could never have had an opportunity of meeting any of my family—'

'Not directly, no, Sir,' Man interrupted gently. 'Yet some years ago in the Park I was a helpless witness to your first son's unhappy and fearful death. You have my sympathy, Sir.'

Abraham Sinclair stared. 'Which?'

Man felt as if he had missed a step. He looked vacantly at the old man looking vacantly at him. The importer's eyes seemed hooded and dry.

'Uh – forgive me, Sir, I should not have – the pain of young Jacob's death must still be with you. I didn't think.'

The room filled for a moment with the shared discomfort of an old and imperfect memory, until Abraham Sinclair waved a hand that sloshed a spray of his drink into his lap.

'Jacob, yes – a tragedy, Sir, that yet lies next to my heart. He should never have been with her – there.'

And that was all. The ageless eyes found their focus in the present once again.

'You will learn something of my family, Mr Man, though you will need to meet with only a very small part of it.

'My present wife, whose name is Anne, is now in her forty-seventh year. She is an ideal helpmeet for a man of trade, and she keeps a good house.

'I have three daughters, Sir – three of the most dutiful girls any man could ever be able to conceive.

'Hester is forty-eight this year, though her age does not dissuade her from showing all due reverence for her stepmother. She is a serious and a well-read girl, though something overrun with the hypochondria and forced to keep herself to her bed.'

The old man stopped to take breath and to roll the liquor lovingly round his tongue. It was now that the watchman first noticed the network of striations at the end of the nose.

'Then there is Philippa. She is thirty-two. An intensely emotional young girl. She still mourns her – my son that was killed, Jacob.

'Sophia is my youngest girl at twenty-seven. A twin to her dead brother, but she always had a will of her own. Some have called her headstrong – not in my hearing – but she could do far worse, I think, than to model her manners after her – family.'

It was stark madness of Man to say it. Maybe it was the usquebaugh: already the harshly angled body of Abraham Sinclair appeared to him foreshortened, blunted, shifting nearer at every quickened throbbing of Man's own heartbeat.

Or maybe it was the profound unease and frustration that Man was feeling, sitting in this unhappy room across from an old man whose only object in life was to grasp and to hold.

Or it could have been the importer's mathematical way of enumerating and classifying the members of his family, much as Sarah Man had woefully cited the original shop and price of each household item her husband had been forced to pawn.

Whatever the reason, Man now baldly interjected: 'And as yet none of the girls has married?'

The oddest thing was that Abraham Sinclair calmly refused to admit the existence of the question. There was simply no reaction at all, perhaps only a further deepening of the inhuman eyes.

'Now I have two sons as well, Mr Man. James, who is now twenty-five, and Walter, who is twenty. And no father could ever have been blessed with better or more loyal sons whose every waking thought is turned towards their family and their father's work. The elder directs the transfer of the goods at the river – I am not much there myself, of course – and the younger helps me take care of the papers and ledgers in this room. Both boys have almost as sure an eye for the business as their father. They are a tribute to the name they carry.'

'And would it be possible, Sir, for me to speak with James himself tonight?'

It was Man again, disrupting the settled flow of the other's neatly arranged speech.

'He is not – here just now. But he will return again well before midnight.'

'Do you think it safe that he should be abroad by himself, considering—'

The old man grew restive.

'There should be no danger tonight, I think. He is at the home of his – his intended bride. And he has a man to come home with.' Sinclair rose to his feet. 'But both our pipes are cold, Mr Man. I'll fetch some more.'

Man watched him hobble over to the table, busy himself noisily with the cleaning and refilling, bustle about with the fire. A curious expense of energy, accompanied by a few furtive and calculating looks at his guest.

The old trader worked hard at getting his pipe well-started, his gaunt cheeks caving inward at every suck. They showed few teeth left.

'You have doubtless seen the advertisement.' Sinclair puffed the words out. 'Mr Psalmanaazaar is a thorough fellow, if nothing more. What do you think on it?'

'The same as you, Sir, if I am not mistaken.'

'And what do I think, eh?' The ashen lips parted in the corpse of a smile.

'Well,' said Man slowly, 'I supposed you considered the advertisement as a very real threat to your son's life. Else why do I sit here with you now?'

Abraham Sinclair seemed to accept this reasoning, although he looked a trifle disappointed, as though his private joke had failed to register.

He relaxed back into his chair, letting his pipe burn itself out in his hand. The incredible eyes were half-lidded and trained upon the centre of the watchman's chest. Man could hear the distant rasping of the ancient lungs.

'I am a man of substantial wealth and power in this city, Mr Man. You yourself could never know how much – will never know. It has taken me most of my life to make what is mine, and I still intend to build it further and preserve it in the future. There is nothing that can stand for long in the way of this.

'When a man has sons, he naturally expects them to work at his side. It is my good fortune to have begotten two that gladly follow my lead and contribute as much as they can to my work. They both conform perfectly to the wishes and the needs of the Sinclair family.'

Man interrupted. 'And they mean to share the business between them, after you yourself are gone, Sir?'

The watchman witnessed something like a haze, a momentary suspension, that started up in the eyes and rippled outward into the entire body. He was watching a full suit of armour that was, for the space of a breath, emptied of the living form within it and left sitting vacant.

Then the old man was back.

'And now one of my enemies – I have many, Mr Man! – has thought to wound me through my son. They know there is no other way to get at me, so they come on me from behind.'

The light of the candles was waning, and Man had to peer into the shadows.

'You are frightened, Sir?'

'Yes. Yes, of course.' But Man could tell the word was new to him.

'And your son?'

'James? No, James is young, and the young are not wise enough to fear.'

'Has he enemies of his own, do you know?'

'He is not important enough to have enemies, Mr Man.'

'Perhaps his bride, then,' Man said carefully, feeling his way. 'Perhaps, as in the case of your first son, the young lady has known another man who—'

'No, no, no!' Sinclair waved it aside. 'There is nothing of that here, nothing of that. It's at me they want to strike – at me alone!'

'Yet the date printed in the advertisement lies so close to your son's coming marriage . . .'

Man was not quite ready for the raking look of distrust that reached out at him from the darkness.

'Who told you that? Mr Psalmanaazaar?'

'No, a friend.'

Abraham Sinclair settled back into his chair, still suspicious. Man kept pressing him, although the watchman himself could not have said why.

'Then the threat may have come from some man in your own business, Sir – some worker at the river warehouse, perhaps – who fears he may already have been uncovered.'

Now the old importer's hands were gripping his bony thighs.

'What are you talking about, Sirrah?'

'I had thought, Sir, that you suspected some deficiencies in your goods earlier this year and that you hired the thief-catcher from Little Turnstile on that account.'

This was too much for him. He was on his feet in an instant and over at the table in another, fumbling with the box of tobacco. This time he had taken his own pipe only.

The watchman was not surprised. He knew now that Abraham Sinclair was the sort of man who hired his underlings in the same way as any freeman of the city hired street-porters. They would be paid for their strong backs and for their agility in following orders. They would be ordered to talk as little as possible – not to think – and certainly not to pry into the affairs of the master's family. Man had broken the first rules of the tractable servant: he knew too much, and he wanted to know even more.

And just now he was glad that he had.

Sinclair took a light and sat down again, smoking fiercely. He pulled in three or four huge lungfuls of smoke that set him coughing and spitting into his withered lap. When he had finished, he looked a little older.

'It appears to me, Mr Man, that you have missed the cushion in a bad way. Wrong as wrong, Sir! If I sent Mr Psalmanaazaar out to find you and bring you to me, it was only that you might work to protect my son – not to worry yourself needlessly with what cannot concern you.'

'And you don't care to know who might want to kill your son, or why?'

'Can't be known; and even if it could, it would hardly profit a man much to know it.'

'What is it you want of me, then?' Man asked, although he already knew the answer.

Abraham Sinclair gave the watchman a waxy, sickly smile that Man was to remember for a long time.

'Why, simply to carry my son, James, safely past the twentieth day of this next month. Nothing more nor less, Mr Man. For which I will pay you the sum of seven pounds precisely – on the twenty-first.'

The wages of a good bricklayer.

'When should I start, then?' asked Man. 'Tonight?'

'Oh, I think tomorrow will be soon enough. He runs no danger tonight. I will ask you only to accompany him in the streets to and from his work and to take up a place near him at the warehouse. And, of course, to carry a pocket pistol about with you at all times.'

'I have none, Sir. And I am much more used to my watchman's staff. It has always served me well enough before.'

'Nevertheless, I will lend you one of my own. And a good sword as well. My son is worth more to me than your own personal desires, Mr Man.'

'Of course, Sir.'

Standing up again, this time with that indefinable finality that signals the end of an interview, Abraham Sinclair looked sternly down at the watchman.

'You will understand, Sir, the grave responsibility that I am entrusting to you. The loss of my son would cost me more than you could ever imagine. I leave his fate in your hands.

'Remember this, too: his safety is now joined together with your own. Should you fail me, there is no man in this city who would not speak your name with hatred. As for myself, I would take it as a lasting personal injury. And I am a man that neither forgets nor forgives.'

As Abraham Sinclair was making his way impressively towards the door, the watchman was still wondering about the strange emphasis that the old man had laid upon the word 'cost'.

Man rose from his chair and spoke to the slumped back.

'One thing more, Sir. Does your son, James, agree with you about the need for such protection? If he does not—'

The importer did not even bother to stop and turn around.

'My children, Mr Man, have never known what is the best for them.'

In the hallway, the phantasmal steward materialized out of the wall, flapping Man's bedraggled coat with distaste.

'Mr Walter has just stepped out, Sir.'

Sinclair turned on him.

'To where?'

'Sir, he would not say.'

'By all that's damned!'

He remembered the watchman and stopped himself. Man was out of the house in one smooth motion. He could hear the old nails scratching at the door as it was shut behind him.

Soho Square had by now grown quieter and darker. The clatter of hooves and wheels receding into Sutton Street came to Man as a hidden stirring in the depths of an immeasurable pool. All the light in the square was concentrated in the few lamps set about the bound enclosure at the centre, and even they seemed to have become smaller and more shrivelled than before.

Man headed towards the north side of the square, skirting the solemn railings with their iron points lopped off by the darkness. He could not hear the fountain inside, and he felt again the obscure menace of the place, as if it were in here that the good citizens of Soho Square kept all the night's shadows locked away.

He was well into Charles Street when he finally decided that he was being followed.

Man did what he always did in such cases: he stopped. And when the footsteps behind him slowed and stopped, he turned round and walked back, making as many rough noises as he could. Now it would be his pursuer's turn to decide.

He thought he could hear that decision being reflected in a series of false starts and awkward shufflings, until at last he came upon a reduced figure standing perfectly still at the edge of the road.

'You mean to talk with me, Sir?'

There was almost no light, but the watchman guessed at a weightless, girlish body and a pale and trembling face.

'You are Mr Walter Sinclair?'

Man stood and listened to the breath squeaking painfully in the young man's throat.

'You saw my father.'

Man made no reply; it was not a question.

'You are hired to safeguard my brother, James, are you not?'

'He has received a threat against his life – a public one. You would want him protected, wouldn't you?'

After a silence: 'You talked with my father.'

It was unsettling for Man to talk with someone he could not see and who returned him only unconnected responses. It was as though he were blind and Walter Sinclair deaf.

'Are you frightened for yourself as well?'

Man distinctly heard the clicking of brittle teeth.

'My father is a very great man.'

'One of the richest and the most important in the city, yes,' Man replied. He was starting to get irritated.

'A very great man.' There was a giggle in the darkness, bits of shell-thin glass broken underfoot. 'Yet my father is not as great as Mr Abraham Sinclair, is he?'

Both men heard it at the same time: hurried, staccato footsteps approaching from the square. The chastised steward sent out to bring the wayward son home.

Young Walter Sinclair scurried off without a word, and Man flattened himself against the dank wall. He heard a quick, muted conversation, then the two men running back to the house.

That settled it for Man. He had had quite enough for one evening. He set off rapidly up Charles Street, striding towards the turning into Tyburn Road. He would spend some of the rest of the night at the near-by home of his friend, James Figg, at the sign of the City of Oxford. There was a newly-built amphitheatre at the back of the house, and tonight was scheduled a fight with iron-tipped quarterstaffs, followed by a boxing contest between a Billingsgate fish-woman and a Newgate basket-woman. The last called herself the 'City Championess', and Man did not want to miss it.

He felt in desperate need of a diversion.

Chapter 8

It was neither dark nor quiet at Charing Cross. Almost all the ground-floor windows were glowing, the lamps in the street were beaming a viscous yellowish light out through their dense refracting glass, and the junction itself was crisscrossed by the dancing will-o'-the-wisps of jogging link-boys. Between the buildings surged a gross vortex of noise in which the braying of gentlemen counterpointed the screaming of horses and the crescendo of shrill women's laughter echoed the exaggerated barking of frantic street-hawkers. Nothing stood still, and the vibration of ceaseless motion invigorated the chill air.

It was here that the highest and the lowest of London and Westminster converged. Roving gentlemen's sons surveyed the wares of brassy prostitutes, and powdered ladies leaned out of coaches to stroke the unrolled material of the ogling linen-draper's apprentice. Residents of the foreign quarter to the south of Soho Square steered sobbing relatives towards the Golden Cross Inn. And above it all, the horse of Charles I looked down narrowly upon the disguised churchman scuttling through the warped door of Mr Harris's Bull and Gate Bagnio.

The scene inside Robinson's Coffee-House was much the same, only smaller and more concentrated. In here, slivers of candlelight pinpointed the tables through the dusk of tobacco, men's voices were raw from too much smoke and drink, and the composite reek of coffee and spirits, sweated bodies and yearly washed clothes, made any attempts at normal breathing unimaginable. The continuing thrill of yesterday's Coronation was in the room, but it was not really needed. Robinson's Coffee-House had never lacked for animation. It was a place where things could happen.

It was just the sort of place in which Alice Kettilby, the good baker-woman in Ironmonger Row, would expect to find George Man's scraggly friend, the one she always called the Bastard. Such a man would feel ideally at home in the family of wastrels and castaways which always kept Robinson's Coffee-House roaring into the small hours. And tonight, at least, Alice Kettilby would have been right.

Richard Savage sat at the back of the house at the dirtiest and shakiest table in a roomful of dirty and shaky tables. He was enjoying a pipe with the same disdainful congratulation of self with which some men enjoy total abstinence. Two bottles of wine, one emptied and the other nearly so, stood before him on the table. There was no one with him now, but he was not alone: another sad chair faced his own, and there were glasses and plates for two.

He casually looked round the reverberating room and smiled benignly to himself. He often smiled; the print of it could be read among the other marginalia in his hungry face. It was the quick smile of a man who craved other men's company, the warming bustle of conversation and drink and ample food. But at the edges of it lay something else: the uncertainty of the man who knows how deep his craving is, and that eventually the company must break up, that most of the others would have homes to go to, four walls, perhaps even someone to listen . . .

Savage's eyes stopped at the door and at a lull in the traffic in the cold dark street, then he looked away.

Five or ten minutes later he was joined by another man, a lanky twig of a man who seemed to have too many bones for his body. He was little more than a clothed collection of sharp ends; and as he spilled himself down the narrow stairs at the back of the house and made his way across the room, missing no table with his knobby hips, he looked to be the clumsiest man in all London. But he sighed happily as he piled himself on to the chair opposite Richard Savage.

'You would tip a bottle over from across an empty room, Ned,' Savage said to him. His smile was brighter now, truer.

'Nay, Dick, but these Charing Cross houses are a man's best home, ain't they? They can show what's not been seen in any dream outside a bottle. There's a dame now over to Angier's that's got three of the whitest bubbies—'

'Yes, yes, I have heard some talk of each of them.'

The scarecrow showed his few black teeth.

'But have you been up the stairs here yet, Dick, to see our Mary?'

'Not yet, no.'

'Aye, then! But don't she show for a penny and let touch for a shilling, though!'

Mary Tofts of Godalming had been delivered the year before of the trunk, head, and skin of a rabbit of about four months' growth. The King's own anatomist, Nathaniel St André, had attended her himself and brought her up for further observation at Mr Lucy's bagnio in Leicester Fields.

Savage shook his head at him.

'A vile cheat and an impostor and nothing beyond.'

'Well then, Dick –' the other man closed a milky eye – 'there's some says yes now, and some that still says no.'

They worked away at the wine, and in a very short while Savage called for another bottle and some cheese. The two men talked idly, naturally, the way two men will who have known each other well since their boyhood together.

In fact, Richard Savage had known Edward Bellamy a scant five hours. They had met at one of the noisome night-cellars which were so numerous in Charing Cross, this one most famous for the vast assortment of rodent bites a man could carry away with him in the morning. They had talked a bit and walked the streets, each of them penniless. Then a swift digression by Edward Bellamy into a linen-draper's shop had produced a fine lady's smock and a grave debate at a pawnbroker's a palmful of cash, and the two men had gone to take refuge in the loud main room of Robinson's Coffee-House. Richard Savage had done all the ordering and Edward Bellamy all the paying, but neither had seemed to notice.

Now Savage was taking the measure of the housebreaker's seedy coat over the bowl of his pipe and nodding wisely.

Edward Bellamy picked up a pinch of the sleeve.

'Aye, Dick, this'll be my yawning coat you see me in: it's not had a nap for itself this long time!' He eyed the other man's newer jacket. 'But that one's been napped right recent to my mind, ain't it?'

'A gift from a patron, Sir, rightfully earned.'

'No less, I'm sure, Dick. No less.'

Savage set down his pipe and helped himself to some of the cheese. It took him a minute to smile again.

'I have been looking for you, Ned, these last two weeks together.'

'I'm here then, ain't I? And when I'm not here, I'm over to there.'

'Cracked any good houses lately?' Savage asked cautiously, his eyes drawn to Bellamy's sordid hands. They were all joints and raised knuckles, and they probed for the bits of cheese with a pewter fork as clumsily as a child trying to handle a watery slice of peach. Yet when the cheese was gone, so was the fork – somewhere into the decrepit coat – and Savage had seen nothing at all.

'Well, now, there's good houses and there's good houses.' Bellamy gummed his cheese. 'But the best is them what give you something more than you came for.'

'Yet you may find yourself with something that has great use for another, but none for you.'

The housebreaker looked slyly into his glass. 'All things can be used, Dick. Any man that knows himself ought know that.'

'Papers, too? Private papers? Those are hard to trade for cash.'

'Nay, Dick, not if it be the right thing and the right man. Now everything has someone somewhere what wants it, don't it? And'll pay for it. Find the man, and you've found your business.'

Savage fell silent, looking at his man. He felt dirty being in the company of the housebreaker, deeply sullied, and just a little bit afraid. But he needed him.

The crowd in Robinson's Coffee-House was thinning, but only by degrees. Savage quickly scanned the room, avoiding the door to the street, and summoned a drawer with a flick of his head.

The man was slow and witless, a coffee-coloured mark staining one cheek.

'Do you call, Sirs?'

'Another bottle and two plates of oysters, if you keep any.'

The drawer carried off the plates without noticing that now both forks had disappeared.

Savage uttered his next words as delicately as an old jeweller setting costly stones.

'Mrs Brett, now, keeps a handsome house.'

'Now that's a rum enough one, to be sure, and the mistress of it a jumbling slut, too, by all that's been told me.' Bellamy bent over the table with a leer. 'Do you know the house and the lady yourself, Dick?'

Savage stiffened. 'All men know she is my mother, Sir.'

'But do you know the house, Dick?' Bellamy teased him.

It seemed suddenly quieter where they sat. Savage was staring at the back of the housebreaker's wasted coat.

'I have passed before it enough times of a night, when the street was dark and only the watchmen out. And I have sometimes seen her cross her apartment with a candle in her hand or come to open the window to feel the air. She would look out then, but she could not see me standing where I was.'

'But did you never go in then, Dick? It's far finer in.'

'Once. The door lay open and unwatched.'

'Ah, then she invited you to her table, eh?' Bellamy mockingly slobbered his lips. 'She's said to set one of the broadest in the town, even now.'

'I could not say.'

The oysters and the bottle came, and Bellamy lowered himself to his work. Savage was no longer there.

'I went straight in and up the stairs to her own chamber. I know the window. There were none of the servants about to delay me. Only to see her for the moment, I wanted nothing but to talk with her. But she discovered me outside her door and raised the house against me. I was carried shouting back into the street.'

'Marked you for a house-lifter, did she?' Bellamy gloated.

'More than that! She charged me with—' Savage swore a black oath – 'she said I meant to murder her!' Somehow the verb seemed to be too big for his mouth.

'Now that's hard, Dick. That's a hard dun, that is.'

It was just now that Savage realized that the housebreaker was nastily playing with him. A quick trio of drinks brought some new colour into the poet's narrow face, and he angrily shoved his own plate of oysters across the table.

'Now hear me. This time last month it was that Mrs Brett's house was robbed of some notes and some cloths – and, as I have heard, an armful of private papers.'

'Was it, then?' Bellamy casually reached for the oysters.

'I think you know it as well as I!' Savage's breath came as if he were toiling up a long hill. 'Now one man has told me that among those papers lay one in the hand of the Earl Rivers himself. A note perhaps – nothing more – but legal enough for all that. Something he penned in 'twelve during his last days to provide for each of his natural children. And I, Sir, am one of those,' he added proudly. 'A full six thousand pounds was promised me through my mother's offices. Six thousand, Sir!'

'A neat figure, that.' For some obscure reason, Bellamy was busily pocketing the empty shells. 'But this was – what? – fifteen years back. So where's the gilt gone to?'

Savage frowned. 'Back into the family, I should think. But with the note, I could make them – or her – pay me yet.'

'Oh, the lady'd like that!' Bellamy said wryly. 'But what changed his mind, then? Heard you was nailing shoes together, eh?'

Savage was obviously shocked to learn that the housebreaker knew so much of his history. And ashamed.

'No, it was my mother – my own sweet, loving, poxed bitch of a mother. She – swore to him I was dead!'

Savage had spoken from a long pain, and Edward Bellamy gave a low, wet whistle.

'Oh, now that's a woman would freeze the stones on you. And here was me thinking she was saving that paper all these years just for you.'

This bothered Savage. The senselessness of his mother's holding on to such evidence for so long was a new thought to him. He gave a sudden, reflex jerk as a man does when he snatches up an empty bucket he thought was full. Then he tried desperately to drive the idea from his head with another dose of drink.

The rhythmical patter of the room enclosed them and enclosed the second's disturbance caused by a small man who abruptly scurried out of the door. Savage gauged the spindly figure of the housebreaker who was now sprawled loosely in his chair, digesting.

'Do you have it, Ned?'

'Have what, Dick?'

'The paper of the Earl Rivers,' Savage said mournfully. 'The paper that could save me.'

Bellamy turned serious. 'Why should I have it, Dick?'

'Well, if you don't have it to sell, why in hell have I been making ready to give Bill Merchant a hundred guineas to get it from you?'

The housebreaker was not a slow-witted man, but this took him some time to grasp. By the time he had it worked out, every oyster shell had disappeared from the table.

'A hundred, eh?' he whispered. 'Now there's a mortal sight of distance, ain't there, 'twixt that and twenty-five.'

Savage brushed the irrelevance aside. 'Well, do you have it, or do you not?'

'Eh? Oh, I've got it, that's certain enough!' the other man decided. 'But do you have the money, Dick – not for Mr Merchant, but for me?'

'I – hope to get it before too many days more.' Savage was flustered, but too proud to show it. 'But I should like to see the note first to verify the hand. Do you have it by you at the moment, Mr Bellamy?'

They were interrupted by the appearance of the drawer who took away the remaining plate and walked off with a mystified frown, vaguely searching the littered floor.

'Nay, not with me now. I can't carry everything about with me every time I'm in the streets now, can I? It's safe enough in its own home and only waiting for me to take a bite of your coin before showing its face. Anyway, Dick,' Bellamy leered, showing a mouth that was spaced with what seemed to be lumps of hardened tar, 'between two good men such as ourselves there's got to be a little trust now, don't there?'

Savage shivered and looked away, trying to hope.

Later that night, the small man who had dashed out of Robinson's Coffee-House was walking energetically through the cold dark of Warwick Street near Golden Square, but he was not in a hurry and he was already warm enough.

William Merchant was trying to keep up with the longer legs of another man, a man dressed in a fine three-cornered hat with a well-brushed grey surtout and tight breeches and possessing one of the most painfully straightened spines in the whole parish.

The two men were talking, but Warwick Street was all but deserted. They could not be overheard, there was no one to observe them.

At first Merchant did all the talking. His stooped body twisted sideways in sly secrecy and nodded in scraping supplication. His small voice whined weakly between the rows of tall buildings.

Then the other man stopped them both, shook his head just once, said a few short words, and moved them on again.

This time he did the talking. He did not need to look at the street-porter beside him, and the tautness of his body kept a cold distance between them. The sound of his voice was as crisp and dry as frozen straw.

When he had finished speaking, neither man said anything for perhaps twenty paces. Then William Merchant dipped his head briskly, repeatedly, accepting everything.

The steward belonging to the household of Mrs Anne Brett efficiently outstripped the porter and continued down dark Warwick Street alone.

Chapter 9

As the city gradually learned to accustom itself to living under the new King and in Dartmouth Street Hester Wells kept calling more and more deliriously for the son who had refused to come, George Man filled his days with the tedious safeguarding of Abraham Sinclair's elder son and his nights with a vacant longing for the company of his missing wife.

Every morning found Man stamping his feet against the cold ungiving stones of Soho Square at six o'clock. Each day seemed more freezing than the last, and darker. Alone in the square, Man wrapped his greatcoat more snugly about him and waited for James Sinclair to come out. The pocket-pistol weighted his coat too low on one side, and the short bilbo which he had borrowed from James Figg stung his thigh with cold on the other. In spite of the orders of Abraham Sinclair that he carry a longer sword, Man had held out for something he could hide beneath his coat. He needed the work, the money; but he was determined not to parade himself about the town like a damned fool.

The young man came out of the house at the same minute every day; and every day the two of them walked wordlessly down the lifeless streets, making for the warm and glowing island of a coffee-house in Wych Street. James Sinclair smoked and read yesterday's news-sheets and drank three bowls of bitter coffee. He never drank spirits before a day of work; but Man had early on made a silent arrangement with the proprietor, and the watchman's coffee came to him liberally sweetened with brandy. Then he sat and drank and warmed himself, while the trader's son casually ignored his existence. Man had tried to talk to him once or twice, but he had been answered only by the crisp turning of a page.

Then on to the warehouse, ideally located in Beer Lane, Thames

Street, at the back of the Custom House. There, Man invented a place for himself in an unused corner and tried to stand out of everybody's way. It was never hard for him to keep James Sinclair in view: the young man's authority intruded everywhere – down towards the river and the lightening ships, between the shoulders of sweating workmen, into the loaded carts. Man's chief labour was to stand clear of Sinclair's sharp, efficient eye. Every time he passed, the young trader seemed visually to measure the watchman's niche and frown in exasperation at the costly waste of floor space.

Dinner was a rush down to a riverside tavern, then back up to the warehouse for more of the same. At the end of the day, they would half-run back to Soho Square, still exchanging the fewest possible words. Man was never invited in.

The routine rarely varied. Twice or three times in the week, James Sinclair had to hurry by carriage to distant parts of the city to oversee a shipment or to suffer the hour of hard drinking that went with important negotiations of merchandise and money. Man had never known anyone who could stretch out a single cup of weak ale for so long.

At such times – in the street, the tavern, the parlour – the watchman was the unusable appendix, the third thumb. Man often saw people he knew in the streets or the coffee-houses who would look inquiringly his way; then he would don his most impassive expression, trying his best to pretend he was alone or elsewhere.

Sundays were the easiest. These were the days that the entire Sinclair family spent as a silent mass indoors, and Man was free to sit with Sarah in her father's house or walk with her through the frozen beauty of St James's Park. Neither of them talked much: they were both too caught up in their own thoughts. But for each of them, simply knowing the other was nearby was enough.

It was odd, but the part the watchman liked best about the thankless work was the slow hours of his self-conscious vigil at the warehouse. He had always liked the intensely physical atmosphere of such places, ever since those days long ago when he had played at castles in his father's crowded brewery. He liked the crude simplicity of the workmen, the lifting and hauling and joking and swearing, the unthinking labour of men moving goods. At Abraham Sinclair's warehouse, Man saw crates of bottles with markings he could not read, splintered casks spilling fragrant tobacco or snuff, overfed sacks of rustling coffee, living bricks of cheese. The men who worked there were no different from those he was used to meeting in the night streets – only more honest. They worked with their backs, ate when it was time to eat, drank when they felt like drinking. They had nothing at all in common with the rich house in Soho Square, though they were the men who had helped to build it.

The only foreign element in the scene, Man thought, was the one that kept it all together: the tall, stalking, calculating figure of James Sinclair. A fair young man with skin like unskimmed milk, he had all the bestial energy of his father; but in the son it was neatly channelled, made subservient to ambition, chilled into effectiveness. He would do nothing that could not pay him; he would fear nothing, because all things could be bought or bartered for. Distinctions of birth or class meant little to him. He knew he was better than most other men in the city: the proof of it lay in the weight of his purse.

It did not take Man long to learn the workmen's opinions of the Sinclair family.

'Mr James'll never bow his head for the washing! He'd pinch the blood out of a fart before he'd spend it!'

'Struts round here all the day like a blind crow in a gutter! If he thought animals could do the work any cheaper, why, he'd have 'em! And leave every mother's son here standing down on the Custom House Key with his hands on his ballocks and spitting at the ships!'

'Father Abraham? Well, some say he spends his time to home, gatherin' up his crumbs. But don't you believe it, Sir! He's haler'n you or me! No, it's pickle-me-tickle-me he's playin' at over there, to my way o' thinkin'!'

The watchman heard that none of the workmen, not even the oldest, had ever seen Abraham Sinclair, much less met him. Before James Sinclair had come of age, the warehouse had been supervised by a series of foremen brought in from outside the family – men, for the most part, who had been eased out of their own businesses by the Sinclair network. One ageless workman, crippled by hernia and gin, thought he could remember seeing the old master once sometime before King William – 'come marchin' into here like the old King himself, his near hand set on the glowin'est sword you ever saw!' – but then, the more he thought on it, it could like as been someone else. Yet all agreed that, for more years than any of them could count, the patriarch of the business had given all his time to his mysterious ledgers and to welcoming his more distinguished sellers and buyers into his home in Soho Square.

There was one thing Man learned from the workmen that suddenly sharpened his interest. A year or more before he attacked and killed Jacob Sinclair, William Hawksworth had worked at the warehouse in Beer Lane. Some of the men insisted that Hawksworth had not quit the work, he had been removed – by order of Abraham Sinclair himself! He had anyway been a shoddy and grumbling worker, more often drunk than able. But Man thought he could begin to see just a corner of a possible reason for the senseless assassination of Abraham Sinclair's first son, and he felt that he wanted to keep hold of it whatever might happen to the second.

Of the occasional visitors who came into the warehouse, Man took little notice. Almost all of them were full-bellied gouty men of business, perfumed with wine and powder and success. The watchman kept them in sight and later learnt the names and a little gossip about each of them. They were too oily and deferential to pose any immediate threat to James Sinclair, but Man guessed that none of them would hesitate to hire a circle of brutal street-bullies or a single good man with a sword.

One morning towards the end of October, Man noticed a pair of legless, triangular shadows lying in the bright dust of the open doorway. They belonged to two young ladies who stood bewildered in the middle of the running yard. The faceless one Man at once dismissed as the maid; the other – blonde, open and natural, pretty in a childlike way – was obviously the girl in charge. Because she showed no physical similarity to the Sinclair family,

Man made a guess, and he was right. This was Patricia Windbush, the intended bride.

The girl finally cornered James Sinclair long enough to talk to him. She chattered on in a high bodiless voice, speaking into the base of the young man's throat, while he kept his eyes roving critically round the warehouse. She was voluble with excitement, and he was only too used to it. At last, a keen canine whine came into her voice; it could have shivered fragile glass, but it had no effect at all upon the constantly occupied trader. He automatically pried her white palms off his chest and diverted her in the direction of the watchman.

So perfectly did Patricia Windbush fulfil Man's every expectation that it was like having to suffer the same conversation twice over. She thanked him breathlessly for his loyal watchfulness; he assured her that he was only too glad to help. She could not imagine who could ever wish to harm her dear James; he murmured that it was probably nothing more than an empty hoax. She would spend every day in terror and every night awake; he promised it would soon be over. For every word of the watchman's, she had ten. Patricia Windbush was an animated and emotional, intelligent girl whose greatest misfortune would be that she would never be able to find anyone else to take her seriously.

Man watched her skitter out of the warehouse, trailing her maid behind her like a least favourite sash. There was something more to the girl, Man decided. She realized how good the match was that had been made for her. When she had spoken of the danger to James Sinclair, it had been more of deprivation than of loss. She's found the butter, thought Man, without even bothering to look at both sides of the bread.

Talking of the advertisement, Patricia Windbush had looked frantically round her at the active warehouse like a child let out into the busy street after a long illness. She obviously suspected one of the workmen, or all of them together. They were dirty, loud, ungentlemanly and vulgar; and as she watched them heaving at a crate or trundling a barrel, she could imagine any of them darkly planning a violent robbery of what would soon be hers.

But the watchman knew them by now, knew them as men can

only come to know one another by drinking and eating and laughing together. Besides being too unlettered for the cleverness that lay behind the advertisement, the workmen were of that sort to whom wealth and influence would come only as an incomprehensible burden. They would be put off their feed, obliged to sicken themselves drinking womanish wines, made to dress themselves up like any prancing backdoor usher! What would become of their midday rest, their beery evenings with their friends, their nights of untroubled sleep? They had the everyday example of James Sinclair to contemplate. None of them liked the young man, but none of them seemed actively to hate him. Yet which of the workmen would ever want to become something like that?

For the same reasons, the watchman was soon satisfied that the goods missed from the warehouse in March could not be laid to the workmen or to any of their friends. The limits of their pilfering extended only to the odd bottle slipped inside the breeches or the handful of tobacco stuffed down into one stocking. They had neither the imagination nor the need to siphon off careful bits and pieces with a long-range view to increasing the thievery gradually to major proportions. The men knew very little of the shortages, and James Sinclair himself was not talking. The watchman had no way of knowing if the thefts had continued or been resumed, until he had the chance of learning a little more from a new and unexpected source.

On the first Thursday in November – a surprisingly mild and warming day – a whispered rumour ran among the workmen that *she* was come to visit the warehouse again. At first Man was in dread of another mechanical conversation with the sugary bride-to-be; but just as he had made his way reluctantly to the boarded corner that James Sinclair used as an office, one of the younger men gave him the name: 'Sophia Sinclair'.

She was small and pale with a kind of beauty that Man could only think of as concentrated, distilled. She, too, had inherited her father's forcefulness, the purest essence of it. She stood with her compact body almost crouching forward, as if she always kept herself ready to advance or attack. Even the face she thrust ahead of her, proudly free of patches or powder, held a demanding solidity behind skin that seemed as light and open as foam. Man disliked her at first sight – he had never cared for the craftiness of certain strong women – yet it unnerved him to think that his disapproval would make absolutely no difference to the girl herself.

Sophia Sinclair was talking to her brother, and this time he was listening. They stood together in the middle of the floor and let the warehouse work around them. From a distance, Man had no way of guessing at what they were saying. They did not appear to be arguing, yet neither was smiling.

After the slightest hesitation, the watchman stepped forward and positioned himself almost between them.

'Mr Sinclair?'

It might have been Man's imagination, but he thought it took some seconds for James Sinclair to tear his attention away from his sister. And when he finally looked at his protector, he seemed suddenly short of breath.

'Yes? What is it, then?' He glared at the watchman, then turned back to Sophia Sinclair. 'This is the man I have been telling you about, he whom your father has hired to protect me from my shadow.'

There was a false condescension in his voice that Man had already got used to – and a guarded uncertainty that sounded new to him.

The girl squinted at Man, said, 'He might have chosen something better,' and looked away. The watchman felt as if he were a belated consignment of stale cocoa-nuts.

Man ignored the cut and thought fast.

'I mean to step out into the street for some minutes,' he said to the brother, 'to scout the road and the rear of this house. I trust you will be safe enough in here until I am back.'

The young importer gave Man a strange look – half proud and half haunted – and whispered: 'I've no doubt at all that I shall, Sir.'

Neither of the Sinclairs watched the broad back and the hard shoulders stalking out of the warehouse. Man did not look back.

The girl stayed on with her brother for another half-hour. They bent their heads together over the working ledgers, blind and deaf to the muscular effort going on about them. Sometimes they worriedly shook their heads in unison, twice the brother muttered a curse, and once Sophia Sinclair took a slip of paper from her dress and handed it to her brother without unfolding it. They could have shouted in the warehouse and not have been overheard, yet they spoke as quietly as children speak in bed at night.

When Sophia left, she left without saying goodbye to anyone. The workmen looked up for a moment, grimaced, and exchanged uncomplimentary murmurs.

She turned up Beer Lane, meaning to return to Soho Square by way of the slightly less crowded and fetid Tower Street and then through the relative safety of Cornhill and Cheapside. She had no real need to be cautious: her walk was that of a young, strong animal, confident of its youth and strength, almost running ahead of itself to clear a way.

Swerving aside to avoid the complaining of a loaded cart down Tower Street brought her into the enfolding fumes of a dark, ripening fish-shop at the opening into Black Swan Court. Leaning up against the stone wall, merging with the grime of it, stood a frayed and moulding beggar, a broken pantile held out before him as a plate. He kept his head tilted stiffly downward as if he were sleeping lightly; but his red eyes were opened wide, working the street, and his scratched voice kept repeating like clockwork, 'Farthing for an old soldier, here. Farthing for the soldier.'

The girl was forced to brush almost against him as she passed, skimming herself through a rich breath that made the fish-shop smell fresh.

When she was level with him, the beggar raised his voice a notch and thrust out his tile to block her way.

'Penny here, Miss. You can spare it.'

The arm and the voice broke the girl's quick stride. She half-looked at the beggar.

'Work for it,' she said acidly, 'like your betters!'

'Ah, that's a cold word, that is – work! A word that can break a man's back.' He rattled his tile and peered at her slyly. 'You don't want to be hard with a poor old soldier now, do you – Miss Sophy?'

This had the desired effect of persuading the girl from moving on.

'How do you come to know my name, Sirrah?'

'Well, I knows what I knows, you see. And what I don't – I find out.' He scanned the lively street. 'Now if it's work you're wanting of me, Miss Sophy, I think I can work some newsmongery for you that will pay your time.'

'What news could you know, man, that would profit me to listen to?' the girl asked sceptically.

The beggar grinned, showing inexplicably bright teeth.

'Well, now, I know that there's three butt of the best Hermitage that're promised today to the Black Horse Tavern from Beer Lane that will never see the door of that house in their lifetimes.'

'This is naked nonsense,' the girl sneered, but with a trace of genuine surprise. 'They will be there even now, I'm certain, unless the cart has lost a wheel.'

'Lost its way, most like. Else why should it be rolling down the Ratcliff Highway, if it's bound for Charing Cross? 'Tis a painful long way about, eh?' The beggar relished the game.

A cork faced countryman drove his grunting pig against the girl's flaring skirts, but Sophia Sinclair took no notice.

Finally she said, 'You lie, Sir. I know my father's business better. This earns you no coin from me.'

'Ah, perhaps not, then, perhaps not.' The beggar appeared to give it up. He lowered his tile an inch. 'But do you know your brother's as well, Missy? Or was it only the ghost of James Sinclair that I spied early this morning ordering the cart off that way himself?'

Sophia's clear brow suddenly twitched with a tic of worry. She stared hard at the dingy beggar, then glanced down Tower Street and snapped a shilling into the tile in his hand.

'You saw nothing. Do you hear? Nothing!'

Wondering, the beggar watched the girl scurry off the way she had come, until he heard another coin dropped on top of hers.

He turned to the man who had just stepped out of the dark doorway of the fish-shop.

'Aye, you look to know the maid better than she knows herself, George.'

'No, Joseph,' the watchman answered thoughtfully, 'only a light touch of the bamboozle – and a lucky guess.'

Man's chest was aching with a sharp cold by the time he got back to the warehouse. He had run better, he thought, only last year. But the Sinclair girl was a flying walker, and she had had a start on him. And he wanted to get back in time to witness her second meeting with her brother.

He slipped into the restless mass of workmen, straining his eyes sideways into his skull to see the two Sinclairs where they stood and talked together. The girl was angry, accusing, spitting words out at her brother and biting them off. Once, she waved harshly towards the doors leading to the street. James Sinclair did far less talking, but he shook his head constantly – first disbelievingly, then frantically – and he ended by tossing his hands up and out, then letting them fall helplessly to his sides. This final gesture seemed to satisfy his sister, and the two of them finished by kissing each other goodbye. The brother even walked Sophia Sinclair part of the way to the door.

Man was watching her as carefully as a mother watches an ailing child. And he saw it. Just as she was passing through the doorway, she turned her head and directed at her brother's back a single look – of suspicion, mistrust, fear. Then she was gone.

It all proved nothing, of course. But it gave the watchman a little bit more to think about.

Yet, oddly enough, as he moved to rejoin James Sinclair, Man was not thinking of the importer's family at all. For no reason, a spill of red wine on the floor had suddenly reminded him of something that touched him far more deeply, of a talk he had had last night with his unhappy friend, Richard Savage. Man knew that Savage had a tragic history behind him, but the watchman was afraid the worst of it might only now be beginning.

Chapter 10

Man and Richard Savage had sat up too late in the watchman's rooms and drunk too many cups of burning gin. The young poet had sat too close to the red fire, and the baking heat of it had turned his face into a moving, ruddy mask.

They had talked of Man's conversation with James Gregory.

'Well, your porter need not worry for his friend any longer. He's out of it now,' Savage had said calmly, liberally basting himself redder with drink before the fire. 'I've met and talked with the housebreaker myself – now there's one you have to meet, George. A walking advertisement for a screaming farce, that man is! I thought myself lucky to have escaped him with my breeches still adorning my legs. But he knows which street is which, and I've no doubt that he's got the paper noting the legacy left me by my father. I can't see why I should need to trade through any other man when I can deal just as well with Bellamy direct.' The young man had looked more lively and hopeful than he had in years. He had waited for recognition and wealth for so long that he was convinced they must make him happy.

'Does Merchant himself know of your new arrangement?'

Savage had been surprised. 'No, I don't think so. Why should he? What can it matter?'

'No reason. I was only wondering if it might not set his back up a bit, finding himself left out of it.'

'Hmm. That's possible, I guess. But every man's got the right to shift for himself as best he may, has he not? And I'll tell you, George, I feel better the farther I am away from your porter's cholerous friend. He's the man to hit you low and hard and from behind, leaving you with nothing but a broken back.'

As the night lengthened, the two men had turned to other, more personal topics. Man had mentioned the continuing sufferings of Sarah and her mother.

'I can feel that, George. Tell your wife, will you, that I will pray for her mother and try to visit soon.' He had bent to score the fair skin of his forehead with his fingers, leaving the scarlet marks of them there. 'I know what it is to lose a mother, though not to death,' he had faltered. 'Even after all the pain and loneliness she has lent me, nothing has changed in my sight. I love her still, George. I am a part of her.'

It was this that the watchman had always valued most in Richard Savage, this hidden capacity for rising above his own troubles to a true caring for the unhappiness of others. It showed a natural decency and a potential for greatness in the young man that no one could help but admire, even though he so often seemed determined to let the best of himself go sadly to waste. And there was, too, the poor man's constant returning to a single subject.

'Yet have you thought, George, of what might be coming to you, should the good woman die? The sign-painter's pretty well-flushed these days, is he not?'

But Savage's best qualities were never active for too long. By the time the fire broke up into bloody flags and the bottles of gin emptied, Man had seen the poet drop his face helplessly into his shuddering hands.

'What's to become of me, then? Where can I go from here? Sometimes I don't know if I can go on – ought to go on. Did you know, George, that until my seventeenth year I was called Richard Smith? And now I am Savage. Who can I be next, do you think? Sometimes I feel myself standing inside a large circle of men who are all named Richard Savage: one, a gentleman well-born; another, a poet, a playwright; a third, a hapless beggar; the fourth, a hated bastard. And I am imprisoned in the centre of them all – No Man – who can do nothing to save himself. Nothing.'

And then in a voice so small it was no voice at all: 'I need a hundred pounds, George, to give to Bellamy. I – have a little. A very little.'

'It will be found you.'

Savage had sat motionless, grinding his palms together. The last of the fire had deserted his face, leaving it pale as snow, and had settled into his weak eyes. It had fired the tears.

Chapter 11

Richard Savage could no longer hide from the truth: he was lost.

He had hurried in from Richmond where he had been working hard on a new poem in a confining room rented upon trust. Now he was hurrying towards Westminster to discharge another room there which he could ill afford. The letter had found him this morning: he would pay the debt today or the constable would be called and his meagre belongings held. He could not stand another loss.

The weather was like ice. There was a chewing wind. Savage was tired and frozen, giddy from hunger, on edge. He was almost sure he had a fever. More than once, as he had approached Westminster from the south-west, he thought of turning back. But each time the imagined warmth and company of a city coffee-house, and the dark loneliness of the room in Richmond, made him bunch his coat more tightly at his throat and lower his head into the cutting wind.

He had come up the King's Road all right and through the short cut of Castle Lane; but instead of keeping on straight into Petty France, a grunting set of pigs had flustered him into veering off into Little Chapel Street. Then the premature November dark and a scuffling fight between two butcher's apprentices had sent him up Torment Hill and on into Dacres Street, until he finally stood sweating and bewildered in the maze of lanes and alleys surrounding the Great Almnery. He had stumbled most of the way, fallen once or twice; and in the clinging dark and amongst the moaning and complaining shadows, he began to wonder feebly if he would ever manage to find his way out.

Somehow – he could not have said by what chance turning – he found himself at last in Black Dog Alley opposite Dean's Yard. He had a raking thirst, the kind that has its own flavour, and a wandering head. He fingered the few coins in his pocket, then, shaking his head resignedly, he stepped down into a tavern he knew for a warm bottle of wine. The room was busy, but for once Richard Savage chose to drink alone.

An hour later, as he was passing through the Broad Sanctuary in front of the Abbey, the sound of his name being called by a pair of voices suddenly tightened the muscles across his stomach. This happened to him almost daily, but he never got used to it. In a moment he could see the two black figures approaching, the incensed creditor and the brusque constable, and then the bleak and humiliating hopelessness of the debtors' gaol. He wanted to run.

Then the two men were on either side of him, and one of them clapt a hand painfully to his shoulder.

'Well! Here's well met, Dick!' shouted the street-porter, William Merchant. 'And a happy chance it is for the three of us together, I say!'

Savage smiled weakly at the small man in the dark. He had carefully been avoiding the porter's company for some weeks, and now he wished even more fervently that he had stayed in Richmond.

'Now I've missed you these times, Dick,' Merchant went on with brittle joviality. 'Where is it you've been keeping yourself, then? Mopping the pot empty with some pocky jade, I don't doubt!' And he prodded his elbow roughly into Savage's upper arm.

'No, I—'

'You won't know Mr Gregory here, but he's as simple and easily done a lad as ever rode and tied his way into London from the country.' Merchant gestured carelessly towards the man standing large and straight on the other side of Savage. There was an exchange of half-bows.

'I am yours, Sir,' came in a strong, clear voice.

Insensibly, the three men began to drift together up King Street. But William Merchant walked just slightly in the lead, and he held the sleeve of Savage's coat gently between two fingers.

The Bastard was feeling even worse than before. His head seemed to float some distance above his shoulders, something inside him was filling his chest with compressed wool, his leg muscles quivered uncontrollably. He walked between the street-porters with the passive lassitude of a distant relative who has been forced into following the corpse of a man he hardly knew.

William Merchant did most of the talking. He was, as usual, bantering and crude, as always pugnacious with drink. But through his fever and confusion Savage thought he noticed something different tonight about the porter, something so small that only a man in a delirium could miss it. What it might be bothered Savage absurdly, it swelled quickly to a monstrous significance, but he did not have the strength to think about it clearly.

It was Merchant, too, who finally steered them towards shelter.

'Here's a loud house to hand in Axe Yard, friends. A cup or two amongst us to start the night. I pay!' He began to stride off commandingly towards the left. When he noticed Savage's hesitancy, he added: 'Hurry on, Dick! You'll still have time to pay the room off later.'

And Savage was too disordered to remember if he had already mentioned his room in Westminster or not.

King Street was congested enough, so that the three men had had to move forward in an elbowing wedge. But the street was nothing compared to the coffee-house in Axe Yard to which William Merchant led them.

The dark-faced proprietor met them at the door.

'Hardly a where to plant your blind cheeks tonight, gentlemen, though I think we've a corner left to stand.'

Merchant moved closer. 'Now one's been promised me, Austin,' he said in a low voice.

Something passed between the two men, and in a minute the company was seated at a table of sorts set up against the wall.

How often in his life had Richard Savage been in a situation like this? He was tired, sick, worried, deeply uncertain of himself. Yet as the wine was poured again and again, as the talk became livelier and lighter, some of its carelessness began to seep into him, and he grew gradually stronger and less troubled. It was not happiness – it was never really that – but the sinking ease of a man who lies down alone in a wide bed after working too hard and thinking too much. Nothing was resolved, but everything was separated from him and somehow made smaller.

Again, William Merchant carried most of the conversation. Tonight he seemed not simply more garrulous than usual, but more deliberately animated, as if he were trying his hardest to instil an artificial conviviality into the others. It was always he who called for another bottle, who filled the cups to overflowing and gestured to Savage to drink. And there was still something more that was unlike him, some tiny anomaly that escaped definition, although now it worried Savage much less than it had before.

The other street-porter, James Gregory, was silent and brooding. He kept pace in the drinking, talked when he had to, but he spent most of his time staring at his friend with a quizzical, anxious expression on his massive face. Anyone watching him would have thought that he was studying, in his slow way, the surprising eccentricities of a total stranger. At times he would wag his head ponderously and look caringly at the man whom they had waited to meet in the Broad Sanctuary.

The night wore on, the carousers straggled out into the dark. At the table against the wall, James Gregory said something about the late hour and the freezing streets. But Merchant shushed him angrily and Savage ignored him completely. As far as the Bastard was concerned, he was at home already.

No one knew the time, but all knew it was late. The proprietor shambled over to their table at a sign from Merchant.

'Are there beds to buy here tonight, my man?'

The proprietor frowned. 'Why no, Bill. I thought you—'

'Then we're out, Sirrah!' Merchant screamed suddenly. 'And a fart and a turd for your house!'

The porter leapt to his feet with a cock's fury that brought a grunt of surprise from the offended proprietor and a scowl of worry into the face of James Gregory. A fistful of coins was flung rattling on to the table, and William Merchant made his way stamping out of the room.

Richard Savage had no say in the matter; he was content to let himself be led. His head had begun throbbing deeply now, a blunt spine of blood growing up the back of the neck and keeping time with every footfall and every slammed door or shouted oath. He was reluctant to leave, because he was always reluctant to leave any place where men were gathered together to forget the dull hours of their daily lives. The street-porter, William Merchant, was in a hurry to get out of the closing tavern – or in a hurry to get somewhere else. And Savage did not want to be left behind, alone.

In the hulking emptiness of Axe Yard, Merchant turned on them with drunken energy.

'If the houses won't keep us, friends, the streets will! We'll follow where they lead us and play amongst them until first sun.'

He marched them off towards King Street. By now, Savage had forgotten all about the angry landlord waiting up for him in another part of Westminster; he followed along with no thought of where he was going. He still walked with the same proud erectness as always, but tonight the fever and the drink made him feel strangely that he could not reach the earth with his legs.

The second street-porter, James Gregory, hung back, a bulk of shadow, quiet and watchful.

William Merchant carried his bleak parade through the late streets with a clapping, excessive joviality that changed him into a type of drunken bantam. He shouted his companions onward, railed bitterly at every closed-up shop, whipped every passing coach on faster with his wild obscenities. He caromed from side to side of the street and ducked his head into every lightless alley, but he still kept them moving steadily northward up the length of King Street. He seemed to know where he was going.

The cold was watering Savage's eyes and he was shaking his head against the knob of pain inside, so he did not see the shaded light and he was through the door before he knew where he was.

There were fewer men in the room this time, and they looked calmer, tireder. The landlady was a soiled woman with a sad face that grew sadder every step she took towards her three new customers.

Merchant was loud. 'We want a fire, Madam! And drink! And the good Mary Tofts herself,' he added with a prolonged belch, 'if she's free!'

'She's not, Sir!' The landlady sniffed at the three men. 'And I'll not have my house open at such an hour to any trio of gentlemen who've nothing better in their pates than an upturned pot!'

'Now Madam, nothing—' began Merchant.

'Madam Nothing is my name tonight, Sir!' answered the landlady. 'And the door you see behind you turns as well out as in.'

'It is bitter cold without, Madam, and I see no cause why we should not claim a piece of your damned fire as much as any other men.'

She stretched out an arm to begin herding them towards the door.

'No man'll see nothing with his eyes so full of drops.'

Savage was standing off to one side with James Gregory and watching Merchant. Such common haggling, he thought, was beneath him; he would rather they simply walk out now and be done with it. Then he saw William Merchant dip his head down like a hen to the corn – this time not to cringe, but to pull out a pouch of money – and he realized suddenly that he had not seen the gesture all evening.

The landlady wilted at once. 'There ought to be enough of a fire left up there,' she said, pointing at a door above a short flight of stairs, 'that some other gentlemen are just to be leaving. But I'll be wanting a three-shilling bowl of punch for the each of you before you settle yourselves.'

Cursing her, William Merchant flung the pouch at her and rushed towards the door. He had vaulted the stairs and was in the other room before Savage and Gregory could start to follow.

When Savage reached the door, he heard Merchant's rough voice taking charge of the room.

'Will ye for once let a man at the fire, by the blood of Christ, and carry yourselves to hell and out!'

Savage could hear the deep ferocity in Merchant's oaths, though he could not think what it meant. He stumbled badly against his own feet at the door and felt James Gregory close up behind him. Then, with his left hand steadying the sword at his side, Savage hurried in.

Chapter 12

It was not simply the uneasy feeling that something might be about to happen. Man had expected to feel that, tonight. And all the circumstances were ideal for making the watchman suspicious and anxious. But if it were only the threat of a subtle danger, he could have dealt with it easily enough. That was his trade; he had always made himself ready for anything.

But this was different, this was something more. It was like being alone in a vast and empty house and feeling that there was something – some grim and final act – happening unknown in another room, right now. And no matter how soon you found it out, it would be already past repairing.

The feeling had been bothering Man all evening. Something was happening, and he had not the slightest inkling of what it was.

It had started when, for the first time since he had begun watching over Abraham Sinclair's older son, Man and the young trader had not made straight for Soho Square at the end of the working day. Instead, James Sinclair had steered them without a word of explanation towards the upper end of St Martin's Lane and into the prestigious main room of Slaughter's Coffee-House. And it was there, seated at the best table in the house, that Man had had a nasty surprise waiting for him.

John James Heidegger had welcomed the watchman with a bark of a laugh that set his jowls into long-lasting motion.

'Mr Maan, Sir!' The vowel opened into a braying Germanic yawn. 'Good to see you again, Sir, and in a work that fits you at last – no, it does! – down to your boots, Sir!'

The man who proclaimed himself the ugliest in England had showed his worst teeth to the watchman and nodded him towards a chair. The Swiss Count was now no more than a healthy sixty, and he would admit only to fifty; but the horrid mask of his face would seem to oblige him to a hundred at the least. The cascading rings of his wig framed a skull that appeared to have enough old flesh adhering to the front of it to make two or three normal faces. Everything sagged, from the hammocks under the eyes to the bladders of the cheeks to the smutty lip overshadowing the crest of the quadrupled chin. There could be no talk of furrows in the skin, because there was so very little of anything else. And these were so deep as to form a skeletal grid for the worn features.

The supper had been arranged as a business meeting to decide future consignments of Sinclair wines to the Opera House. Man had wondered at once who had arranged it, and why tonight. In a few minutes he had understood it was Heidegger's doing, and Man had watched him with a renewed curiosity. The Swiss Count had seemed subtly changed somehow – still audacious and cunning, but with a strange control, as if he were carefully watching himself doing something disagreeable upon reluctant sufferance.

James Sinclair had seemed to be different, too. Tonight he was less rigid and bloodless, more human and open than Man had ever seen him. He had drunk too much at once and talked with Heidegger more about women and the adventures at the Swiss Count's masquerades than about the debatable prices of wines. Sitting with his head thrown defiantly back, ignoring the existence of his preoccupied guardian, James Sinclair had seemed to be glorying in his new recklessness. He was out in the city at night, and he was not afraid.

After the last two bottles of port, they had taken to wandering through the streets arm-in-arm, the watchman following grace-lessly behind. Man had soon lost track of their erratic course: from the tavern in Bow Street where they had miraculously found a still red champagne to the coffee-house in Tavistock Street and the uncounted cups of Madeira malmsey to the chocolate-house in Maiden Lane where Sinclair and Heidegger had finally closed their dealings over broad bowls of thick wine chocolate. All the time Man had kept himself somewhat apart, confused and watchful, feeling as if he were being led through a maddening and pointless labyrinth.

And gradually the strange, rebellious mood had grown upon James Sinclair until he had seemed to become angrier and more distant – not with Heidegger, but with Man himself. The young trader had stalked farther ahead, scraped his chair to the farthest corner of the table, positioned the Count between himself and the watchman and hurried them towards the brightest and busiest part of the room. More than once, Man had been surprised to see James Sinclair glancing at him with a trembling look, almost as if he feared his own hired protector.

They were moving slowly down Thatch'd House Alley and Man was still trying to guess at what might be happening tonight and wondering desperately where it might lead them, when John James Heidegger suddenly pointed towards the opening of the alley into the Strand and started hurrying ahead.

'She's there!'

When Man came to the end of the street, he found the Swiss Count talking with a young woman who was wrapped in too much cloak. She was excessively gay, badly painted, and wore at the left side of her mouth the largest single patch the watchman had ever seen. Her name was Kitty.

Man could hear the wetness of Heidegger's drooping lips in the dark.

'There's a good girl, waiting so long for us to come!' He turned eagerly to James Sinclair. 'This is the maid, Jim, that gives us all so much of herself at the Opera House.'

The four of them moved into the emptying Strand, the girl dividing herself equally between the trader and the Swiss Count.

''Tis cold tonight, gentlemen, cold as a parson's pizzle. But Kitty'll take you to where you can warm it.'

'Your company has heated us already,' said James Sinclair, squeezing her.

She sighed and burrowed more deeply into his side.

Man was trailing behind again as they came into Charing Cross, reminding himself miserably that he and Sarah really did need the money.

The girl took them into Robinson's Coffee-House, where the landlady greeted them with a loud honk of pleasure – all except Man.

'So it's you then, is it? Come back to finish your cruel work, have you? Four years of peace too much for a good woman, eh?'

Man smiled grimly at her. He remembered that it had been exactly that many years since he had been forced to suggest to the landlady that a visit from the constable might be needed to dissuade her from her abusing of young girls.

The landlady wanted to prolong her anger, but James Sinclair impatiently cut her off.

'Let's go in then, can we?'

Rumbling like a passing storm, she took them up a few stairs and into a private room. There was a good fire crowded into a toy fireplace, a square table with uncertain chairs, and for some reason a curtained bed in a far corner. The girl, Kitty, looked first towards the bed, and something unspoken passed between her and James Sinclair.

In five minutes, there were big bowls of punch crowning the table; in ten more, Man was sitting alone with Heidegger and pretending not to hear the muffled exertions throbbing rhythmically in the far corner.

The Swiss Count did his best to make friendly conversation. He bragged of the raging success of his masquerades, of his close connection with George Frederick Handel and the Royal Academy of Music, of how Italian opera was destined to rule England for the next hundred years at least.

'And Mr Handel will be its master, Sir, believe me! Burlington and Marlborough shall tire of their persecutions, and then you will see our triumph.' He slurped his punch and grew even uglier. 'Hah! Who dares say now there's as little difference 'twixt Handel and Bononcini as 'twixt Tweedledum and Tweedledee? Why, the German is a god beside that scratching Romish parrot!'

Man let him rave on alone. What could the watchman talk about with the man who had meanly used all his power in the city to keep him from his rightful work?

After a time, Heidegger gave up on Man and called for more punch. The maid who brought it was a slatternly horse of a girl with the strength of two men. She had a bad cold; after sneezing into the punch, she wiped her nose on the back of her muscled forearm where the hairs were already laid flat and slick. Before she left, she looked across the room at the moving bed and smiled idiotically. Her teeth were green.

When James Sinclair and Kitty finally came back breathless to the table, the drinking and shouting began in earnest. Heidegger trotted out all his most unspeakable anecdotes about important figures in the town. James Sinclair tried to second him with as much loud wit as he could find in the punch, and the girl giggled and gasped in all the right places. It was the kind of occasion which could go on senselessly for hours.

As for Man, he began to show a sharpened interest in the drawing of his pipe and in the sculptured flakes of ash standing up out of the bowl. He might have been bored or angry or sleepy, but he was only waiting.

He was waiting for the girl to jump wailing to her feet and accuse the trader of ravishing her, then draw a dagger out of her cloak and bury it in the centre of his chest. But she did nothing but laugh.

He was waiting for Heidegger to brandish his drained bowl suddenly above his head, swearing vengeance against the Sinclair monopoly and swinging the bowl down crashing into the man's face, driving the shards back into the eyes. But the Swiss Count was only drinking and being almost funny.

He was waiting for James Sinclair himself to say something, do something, that would help to explain the regular twitches of fear in his face whenever he glanced timidly at the watchman, almost as if he must eventually draw his sword against him or run out panicked and alone into the deserted streets. He was scared of something, though he could not be sure what it was. So James Sinclair was waiting, too.

The hours slid by, and Man was wearier than he knew.

And when the end finally came, it was finished in less than a minute, because nothing great takes very long.

James Sinclair was standing near the table, settling the bill with the snivelling maid.

Heidegger and Kitty were swaying at the side of the room, drunkenly trying to sort out their coats.

Man was still sitting behind the table. He was methodically cleaning out his pipe, his mind a blank.

Without warning, the door was kicked open, and a man came striding in towards the fire. He was a small and fiery man, unaccountably angered, wearing no sword. He glared blackly at James Sinclair.

'Will ye for once let a man at the fire, by the blood of Christ, and carry yourselves to hell and off!'

James Sinclair smiled condescendingly at the intruder.

'We've no further use for it. Any *gentleman* would be welcomed to it.'

The watchman took a closer look at the small man without a sword and sighed. Another tiresome tavern argument.

The intruder seemed undecided for a moment, then he crossed quickly to the table.

'We'll be needing this too, then – but cleared!'

He kicked viciously at the table, sending it over square into Man's chest, tipping him in his chair and taking away his breath, spilling the bowls in his face and knocking his head hard against the wooden floor.

Man heard: 'I'll damn you for such impertinence, Sir!'

'You're a damned puppy yourself, and from a family of whores and thieves!'

The watchman struggled to get the heavy table off his stomach. He pulled himself to his knees by the edge of it.

He was about to jump to his feet, when he saw two new men rushing into the room. The first was Richard Savage, looking pale and flurried; the second was the strong and dependable street-porter, James Gregory. The sight of his two friends in the room surprised Man at first, then relaxed him for an instant, impercept-ibly untensed the muscles in his legs. They would help him to settle everything at once.

But then he noticed that James Sinclair had his sword in

his hand and was shouting something at the first intruder and both Savage and Gregory held naked swords, and then the small man without a sword spat in Sinclair's face and scurried round behind Savage, screaming, 'His sword! Jim!' and Gregory made a grab at Sinclair's wrist, while the small man tried to pull Savage back by the shoulders, and then Man saw – quite clearly and slowly – the point of Savage's sword insert itself inch by agonizing inch into the upper belly of James Sinclair.

There was a perfect silence in the room. The young trader looked up at Savage, said, 'You?' then slithered off the sword and fell to his knees, already dripping. Man heard him speak in an almost normal voice, cold and conclusive: 'Then I am a dead man, and was stabbed cowardly.'

Then Heidegger and Kitty screamed together from where they were cowering near the bed, Man was up and stepping over the fallen table, the maid howled. The small man leapt at the pair of wall-candles, and the room went black. There was a scuffling of feet and blows, the whip of a sword and a screech from the maid, and a clattering of men towards the door. A half-rectangle of light and a mess of noise and questioning voices replaced the door. A small shadow pushed a larger one out.

Man suddenly discovered that he could still breathe.

'Richard!'

He struck out across the darkened room, stepping clear of the grey body of the fainted maid. Man met three excited soldiers at the head of the stairs. The landlady was clucking feverishly behind them.

'The two who came out. Did they leave?'

One of the soldiers gabbled something and pointed at the front door.

'I am of the watch, men. You three come with me.'

They forced their way through the flow of customers who were curious to peer into the private room. Man had to fight hardest against the clawing hands of the landlady, as she demanded that he return to the room and make everything all right. But it was probably too late to do anything about that now. Man had seen how far the blade went in.

Outside in the quieter street an idle link-boy told them that the two men had run off towards the Strand. Man paid him a penny for the loan of his light and hollered for the three soldiers to follow him.

The watchman saved his breath for running. He felt suddenly numb and old, as if a part of the chilling night had just worked its way into his chest and head. He was sick with shock and disbelief, stunned by the impossibility of what he had just seen. That James Sinclair should have been killed almost within his reach was disastrous enough; but that he should have been murdered by one of Man's closest friends – with the watchman as the principal witness – was absolute nightmare. It ached beneath the skin and weakened the muscles the way a monstrous dream can stay with the dreamer throughout the day.

And now Man had to catch his friend and take him to be locked up in the nearest watch-house. He had no other choice.

It was painfully easy to find them. There were more than enough people in the Strand who were eager to point out the trail and even to join in the hunt. The watchman waited to hear what they knew, then shoved them roughly aside.

One Tun Alley, Hungerford Market, was a richly-scented, constricted lane leading down towards the river. It had never been lighted by night or cleaned by day, and with the help of the link-light Man could follow the tracks of the fugitives through the papers, the fishtails, and the reeking slush. As he closed in, he could not help dropping his hand into his pocket and gripping the icy pocket-pistol, although he promised himself fiercely not to take it out.

The three soldiers pressed against the watchman from behind. They were unarmed, but grimly determined to make the most of the night's adventure.

From the black well of a warehouse doorway just ahead Man heard an urgent voice, but it was not Savage's.

'You say you felt nothing, then?'

Richard Savage was hunched into a corner, while the small man without a sword stood over him protectively. In his friend's white face Man could find nothing but the stark surprise of despair. There was no meanness, no anger, no fear – only the blank expression of a finally confirmed hopelessness.

Savage looked up, blinking into the glare.

'Do you think, George, we might first try to see the man who owns my room? I have a debt to pay.'

During the long walk to the watch-house which stood in the Strand in front of Somerset House, Savage moved silently in front beside the watchman. He was as erect as ever, only there was a degree of certainty missing from his stride, and his eyes looked at nothing. The other man followed docilely behind, girdled by the three disappointed soldiers.

Man was resting himself. He did not yet want to think about all that had happened tonight. It was still too soon for that; tomorrow would be better.

He would be better, too. Now he could not sort out the many conflicting feelings that were starting up inside of him. He was tired and perplexed and deeply frightened – but he also felt an odd sense of resolution, as if something growing and complicated had finally come to rest.

Who could not have guessed that tonight was the night of Monday, 20 November 1727?

Chapter 13

Whenever Sarah Man looked at her husband in that way, it meant that she was gently impatient with him for his stubborn attachment to some far-fetched idea.

'Yet you say, George, that you saw Mr Savage run through poor Mr Sinclair as certainly as you see me now.'

'I did.'

'And the man had but the one wound on him?'

'Only that in his belly, yes.'

'And your friend, the porter – Mr Gregory: did he not have hold of Sinclair's hand when Richard struck?'

The watchman ironed the cloth over his knee with the warm bowl of his pipe.

'He had – but not, I'm sure, to ready him for Savage's sword. He was only trying to end the fight, as the other fellow who was with them – a Mr Merchant, Jim Gregory's friend in his work – was trying to pull Savage back and out of the room. It could all, really, have been nothing beyond a sad accident,' he finished with less certainty, 'if only the sword had not been thrust in quite so far.'

Sarah winced and fortified herself with some bluish-green Singlo tea.

'Who was it, then, that drew first?'

'That I cannot say, Sarah. It was a mad scene. I was down, you know, and it was all over in a wink. All three men had them out – Sinclair, Gregory, and Savage. But who was first? Most are saying it was Savage; Richard himself, naturally enough, swears it was James Sinclair. But I think no man that was there can be completely sure.'

'Is it important?'

'Of course, wife,' Man answered. 'It might mean the difference between whether Richard Savage walks or whether he dances.'

Sarah Man looked critically at her husband. She was sometimes disturbed by the callousness of his view of things. He was like the surgeon who toys playfully with the amputated limb, because he has seen too many of them.

'Did Mr Sinclair himself say nothing on it before he—'

As she hesitated, Man said bluntly: 'Nothing more than to name Mr Savage – and none other – as his only murderer.'

They were sitting alone together in the parlour of Michael Wells's house in Dartmouth Street, the same parlour in which they had first met. It was a warming day with plenty of fresh sun, the twenty-third of November. Man had just come from Coroner White's sitting at Robinson's Coffee-House, and he was feeling anything but happy. Both Richard Savage and James Gregory had been charged with wilful murder; the unarmed William Merchant, with manslaughter.

The signpainter was upstairs with his wife, who in the last few days had recovered some of her lost strength at the prospect of her son's soon returning home. Man himself felt that the old woman deserved to be told the truth – that Daniel Wells had never had any intention of coming to see her – but the watchman could never say as much to Sarah or her father. Man could not even persuade his wife into coming home with him to Iron-monger Row: she was still afraid her mother might suddenly worsen and die without the family's only daughter by her bedside.

'And you could not ask me, George, to leave my father to face the end alone.'

The situation had rooted something tangled and obscuring between Man and his wife, so they had turned to talk of the murder as to a refuge, a neutral ground. It was something else that concerned them both – but equally – and with none of the jarring overtones of family.

First, of course, was the money promised Man for watching over Abraham Sinclair's son. Man had lost that on the Tuesday morning, when James Sinclair had died in the fine house in Soho

Square. That had been a scene which the watchman's pride did not allow him to describe in detail to his wife. Going for so many months without steady work had already shamed him quite enough.

The entire Sinclair family had been there, the children standing in an orderly rank behind their father with the rest of the household arranged condescendingly behind them. Patricia Windbush, the dying son's intended bride, had been strangely excluded. The only agony in the room had been the wounded man's; the only rage, the father's. And all of it had been directed at the exact centre of the watchman's forehead.

The old man's brittle voice lashing out at him, the impenetrable midnight eyes penetrating him, the accusation and the scorn a palpable weight . . .

Man had stood it as well as he could. It had not been easy: the faceless impassivity of the servants and the children, the hot fury of the father, the body's speechless censure. The rest of the room had been content to let the old importer carry the charge; only once, when Abraham Sinclair had wondered aloud if Man might not have arranged the killing through his friend Savage, did the watchman glimpse in anyone a sensible change. It was Sophia Sinclair: she had looked disappointed.

Could anyone else – anyone who had not been in that room in Robinson's Coffee-House that night – ever see the death of James Sinclair the way Man saw it? Almost the first thing Sarah had said to him this morning was: 'Now you mustn't blame yourself too much for what happened, George. We all know you did your best.' It was the standard consolation that could never console, because it assumed a mistake or failing that for friendship's sake was left unspoken. For his part, Man would not dare to reveal how very little he felt himself at fault in the predicted killing of the young trader.

He blamed himself, of course, for failing in those basic skills of any seasoned watchman: he should have been more alert, he should have moved more quickly, kept his feet under him and his hand near his weapon. But as for the entire set of circumstances leading up to the death, Man felt more mystified than culpable.

He had sensed throughout that he was nothing more than an observer of an unknown and irresistible series of events, that everything had been taken out of his hands. And if he was so dissatisfied now, it was because he had somehow been prevented from doing anything, not because he himself had done something wrong.

While Sarah was upstairs seeing to her mother and father, Man crossed to a shelf and helped himself to some of his father-in-law's dark brown brandy. It blackened his tea, but he thought if he held the cup at the right angle, Sarah need never suspect.

The watchman's wife came back with a heartening report and her usual curiosity to hear still more.

'You've seen Mr Savage then, haven't you, George?'

'I have. Yesterday.'

'Is he well?'

'Oh, he is getting on handsomely, is our proud Richard,' Man replied just a bit too lightly. 'Except for a cold in his head and the missing his books, he might as well be sitting here with us now! There's no holding the man back. He lords it over both the great and the small. There is some talk of making him the next gaoler. He is even now as free from Newgate cuffs as any just-dropped babe.'

'But surely he must need for something, George. It's such a deadly awful place, isn't it? Cold and dark and so loud with rats and all. I could make him a nice warm bread, and there's a good blanket upstairs that you could take him. It'd be no trouble, you know.'

The watchman basked in the simple goodness of his caring wife. Actually, Savage's physical situation in the prison was better than could have been expected. The hasty contributions of his friends had bought him, James Gregory, and William Merchant out of chains and into the comparative comfort of the Press-Yard and secured for them all a steady ration of clothes and beer and safety. It could have been so much worse.

'No, no, wife. He wants for nothing yet. The house is not so completely bad as you may think.'

Sarah showed her disappointment. 'I pray you would not say

the same, George, if it were our – our own dear son lying in there now. I pray you would not!'

Man did his best to reassure her. He knew the surprising depth of his wife's affection for the young poet, and he thought he knew its cause. It was twelve years now since Man had brought home for a solid meal the starving boy who had desperately identified himself in court as 'Mr Savage, natural son to the late Earl Rivers'. At first, Sarah had been as wary of the stranger as she was of all her husband's rescued strays. She barely tolerated such beggars as unavoidable loose ends in the watchman's work. Yet as the years had passed and as Savage had returned time and again to tell his story and to share with them his daily adventures, Man had noticed Sarah's attachment to the young man settling into a firm and lasting love. The same had happened to so many who knew Richard Savage. He was a basically decent and courageous man whom it was easy to pity, but even easier to admire.

Watching his wife worrying herself, Man realized that there was something more. Since the disappearance of their own son, there had been an aching vacancy in their home, a vacuum that Savage had helped in part to fill. And who does not forgive the failings of a son or daughter?

'No, George,' Man's wife said with sudden determination, 'I can't – I won't believe it!'

'Believe what?'

'That our Richard could want or mean to do such a thing.'

'Yet it was done,' Man reminded her.

She waved it aside towards the cold sunlight that was pencilling in through the windows and added a few thoughtful wrinkles to the ones that already belonged in her gentle face.

'Yet didn't you tell me, George, when you first came in here today that you thought the Sinclair lad looked more surprised than afraid at the attack?'

'I fancied as much, perhaps. Who can see or hear a dying man aright?'

'Did Mr Sinclair himself, d'you think, know Richard or Gregory or Merchant?'

'I think not,' Man answered slowly. 'I can see no connections among them either in business or in pleasure.'

'And Richard says he had never even seen Sinclair before?'

'Never in his life. He swears to it.'

Sarah Man came to an unalterable decision.

'Then it could have been nothing more than accident—'

'No, wife, I'm afraid—'

'– else why should any man,' she went on, not hearing, 'want to kill any other man who he does not know from Adam?'

Man was looking off towards the doorway leading to the front hall. If none of the walls had been standing and none of the other houses, he would have been staring straight into the heart of St James's Park.

He said softly: 'He would not.'

'What?'

Turning to look at her, not seeing her: 'Richard did not kill James Sinclair.'

His wife's face soured. 'That again, George? That same weak babble you whispered me at first? I will soon name you "Poll" after Mr Crusoe's witless parrot.'

'Don't be angry with me, Sarah,' Man said weakly. 'But there is so much in this that I cannot understand, and I will not rest with that.'

'The taking of his things, do you mean?'

This had been a recurring theme with Abraham Sinclair: that during the few minutes of darkness in the private room in Robinson's Coffee-House, someone had cleaned out his son's pockets. Some cash, a watch, a valuable woman's ring.

'Not that only, wife. I mean also that where there is no need to murder, there ought to be no murder.'

Sarah Man looked round bewildered at the walls, at the tea-table, at her husband.

'But our Richard – God forgive him! – did kill Mr James Sinclair.'

'And he did not.' Man got to his feet. 'If I hand one man a sword and push another armed man against him and one of them dies, whose guilt is it?'

He had bent to kiss her cheek and turned to go, saying, 'I have a long work to see to,' before she could think what to ask him next.

'But tell me something more! George!'

But he was already gone.

Chapter 14

The old man with a mouth full of black tobacco and an orange handkerchief knotted round his head winked affectionately at the watchman and panted as happily as a racehorse that had won the plate.

'Ah, yes, but ain't it true, though? Whenever good George Man's put to a sad nonplus – when he finds himself lost amongst his Hem's and Ha's – who is it, then, he comes to see to set him back into his bias but Old Father Ward? I swear it cheers the heart – it does! – to see the young ones still so mindful of their elders.'

Man could not deny it. In the nearly twenty-five years that he had known Ned Ward, the watchman had almost monthly made use of the old publican-poet's exhaustive and sensible knowledge of the town. Ned Ward knew Bartholomew Fair and he knew Hockley-i'-th'-Hole; he was as welcomed in Exchange Alley as at the Rag Fair in Rosemary Lane; and there were some who would promise you they had caught him striding gaily through the door of Walpole's house in Arlington Street – and the publican himself would never contradict them. There were very few doors that were closed to the man whom most people still called the 'London Spy'.

The watchman felt at home in the King's Head, Ned Ward's punch-shop and tavern in Fulwood's Rents next door to Gray's Inn. It was a quiet place that could make room for the idling lord or the entertaining merchant as well as the moody street-thief who could not account for the money in his pockets or for the pockets themselves. The shop was well-seasoned – just clean enough that a man would not need to wipe off the rim of the bowl with his cuff and just dirty enough that he could rest his caked boots upon a vacant chair with a shameless grunt. It had that elusive quality of a man's own home: it had stayed in the same location for almost thirty years now, and it had never changed, either for better or for worse.

Man was sitting at a boxed-in table towards the back. The room was full, but not crowded, with a comforting balance of noises: the wordless chattering of cups and pots, the crude exuberance of some soldiers playing cards, the soft humming of a table of churchmen at their pipes. It all provided a perfect, solid background which Man could lean his back against and think and talk. He needed it. His conversation with his wife earlier in the day had started too many ideas in him, too many complications that might lead him anywhere. He knew a part of everything, but he did not know any one thing whole. And time was already working against him: Richard Savage would soon be coming up for trial, and as things stood against him now the watchman believed he must hang.

Ned Ward had just had his drawer bring them two more nipperkins of warm ale and brandy and was now easing it lovingly past the clod of tobacco in his cheek. Man was glad to see that the old publican had not lost his knack for savouring every atom of his daily life. After drinking, the wad was rearranged and a long, black stream let slither to the floor. Man glanced up at the notice hung upon the wall: 'Mop-Money shall be asked of Any Gentleman that Spits outside of the Chimney-Corner.' The message was almost illegible beneath a happy spattering of yellow.

The watchman got down to business. 'Then he'll like enough stop in again tonight, you think?'

'The thief-catcher? Oh, that's sure as a gun, my good friend. He keeps his stall at Little Turnstile, you know, it's not far from here. This is his best place for his night's dram, and I've a three-penny ordinary for those I like the looks of. And we've a kitchen-girl who has near as much flesh on her bones as a Lincolnshire heifer, and the catcher seems to have a taste for it.'

Ned Ward kept looking dutifully round the room as he spoke, but the watchman knew he was interested.

'What time will he come, if he does?' Man asked.

'Well, he'll turn in at, say, misers' bedtime – nine – or something before or after.'

It was now just eight.

'But what's the game then, George?'

'You have heard, I'd wager, of the mean doings into Robinson's, night of Monday last?'

'What? The Sinclair lad that's dead? Aye, I think I might have heard enough of it. But what's your part in it?'

Man briefly described the scene and added: 'And now I should like to see Dick Savage step past it whole.'

The London Spy – the man who said he had studied the city with his bare hands – now wearily shook his head.

'No, there's a work, George, will suck the orange dry before you're done with it. Savage killed him, way I heard it, plain as your pipestem. The Lord, man! You were there yourself, weren't you?'

'I was.'

'And you saw the killing clear?'

'As clear as air, Sir.' Man paused, wavered between embarrassment and determination, then pushed ahead: 'But I do not think Savage meant to kill or knew well what was being done.'

The sage of the Turk's Head tavern nodded over a pout. 'Blind drunkenness, yes, or a moment's helpless madness – well, they might win him something at that.'

'No, neither of those, Sir,' the watchman insisted. 'I mean a man might be led into doing something that he would never want himself to do and that he could not see coming at him until he had fallen full into it. A murder may be as nicely constructed and arranged as any game or dance, I think, even when the players are unsure of the tune. There will be a certain clumsiness, but it can still be made to work.' Man quickly scanned the room. 'You do not keep a chessboard in here, Ned?'

'And will not, my friend, as long as there is breath in this body. I cannot live with any sport that costs a man the best part of an hour to begin. You play it, I suppose?' he finished, fixing Man with an accusing stare.

'Only those times I sit long with my friend, Homer Wolfe. You know him, I think. He says that there is no one game which can show the state of man's life to the full so well as chess. Whether 'tis his own thought or another's, I do not know. But he plays the game like an angel. Now look here, Ned.'

With a boy's eagerness, the watchman suddenly transformed the tabletop into a haphazard field of contest: Ned Ward's cup was slid rudely into his chest, Man's own was set wambling in the centre, and the watchman's pipe was made to stand guard off to the side upon its flat-bottomed bowl.

'Now this cannot give you,' Man hurriedly complained, 'even the roughest image of it. We should need the board, of course, as well as the separate pieces—'

'But I don't care, George!' pleaded the publican.

'– and some marking of the houses in the ranks and the files, if we meant to see the intention of the attack plain. But this will satisfy for now.' Ned Ward started to grumble, but Man cut him short with a show of energy. 'No, first look here, Ned. Look you here!'

The watchman reached across and positioned his companion's cup in an imagined square.

'Now this is your King, Ned.'

'The new George, eh?'

Man did not look up. 'No, his name is James Sinclair.'

The other stopped sucking at the tobacco in his cheek and looked across at the watchman with sudden concern. But Man was almost alone now, following a new rhythm that only he could feel.

He shuttled his own cup about within the middle section of the table.

'And this is my Castle, my Rook, that can be moved straight across the board almost where he will.'

'And his name?' Ned Ward asked, picking up a corner of the watchman's enthusiasm.

'Mr Richard Savage, of course.'

Man pulled his cup back to his edge of the table and aligned it directly across from the publican's. For a moment he frowned over the arrangement, then he took three coins out of an inner pocket. He laid two side by side in front of Ward's cup and one beside it. Now Man was satisfied.

'Your King is now protected, Ned, hemmed about by a trio of his own soldiers. There is no way in, because your King has retreated into a corner. But there is also no way out. The refuge, you see, may be turned suddenly into a trap.'

Man began moving his cup in a straight line towards the protected cup and back again.

'You should know that the threat of my piece can be felt at any distance across the board. But the threat only, not the kill. To get at your King, I must first come close to capture one of your guardians – like this.'

And he stretched over and with his cup firmly slid aside the coin lying directly in front of the sheltered King.

'So your King is now, Ned, in present danger of being taken. And the game is mine.'

In his youth Ned Ward had been a wonderfully quick man, both in body and in mind. He could return a blow as fast as any bully, a word as loudly as any fishwife in Westminster. Now the years had slowed him down considerably, but they had left him with a thoroughness that was deep and settling. He could no longer be the first to start, but he was the one who always finished.

Now he pondered over the configuration of forces on the table with the attention to detail which he usually reserved for new and suspect customers. He measured the situation first with one eye, then with the other; he balanced it with his head; he seemed to weigh it in the pouch behind his lower lip. And then he had it.

Ned Ward was as excited as the watchman had been before, and he smiled slyly as he pushed back Man's attacking cup with his own.

'Now look to yourself, George! You see? You've come too close. My King's a good enough fighter for you, and he'll trade you bite for scratch. So what's your word for this, Mr Jack-a-Lanthorn?'

The watchman was the smug tutor enjoying the surprising wit of his dullest pupil – but then he gestured towards his pipe.

'But here is the Archer – sometimes now called the Bishop – who controls on the diagonal the square on which the Castle is standing. Your King cannot move to put himself in peril by capturing the assassin. As long as the Archer stands here, the Rook can stay where he is – until the King falls.'

The older man sat back with a long sigh, looked from Man to the tabletop and back, then resumed his chewing, his left cheek dimpling in and out.

He pointed. 'So who's the pipe?'

Man busied himself with clearing most of the table before he answered.

'Do you know a street-porter by the name of William Merchant?'

'Eh? Well, I've seen him the odd time, shouldering his load. And he's been in here, once or twice, like the most of them. Height of a ninepin, ain't he? Scarce tall enough to be a complete man, nor short enough to be a monkey? A hot bundle of verbosity with nothing under to hold up the words!' Squinting at the watchman, he added: 'Do you know what I am going to tell you? That boy's last caper will be so far off the ground that he will quite lose all his breath before he comes down again. He's the kind that knows he hasn't a dead man's chance of winning, but you'll be the first he'll blame when he loses. The town's crowded with men of that kidney, and in Newgate they're as plenty as yolks of eggs in brewing time.'

Man was wondering if William Merchant could have known any of the Sinclair family.

'Mr Surlicuff with the Quality? A street-porter that makes his honours with as much grace as a cow might make a wide curtsey? He could never come closer than the cold side of the kitchen, and even that'd be a gain for a man his size.'

The watchman waited for Ned Ward to come to it.

'Still,' the publican wiped his mouth, 'anything's possible when it happens, right? Now if tonight were a month or a bit ago, do you know, George, who the two of us would be? You'd be Bill Merchant himself, sitting with his chin dipping into a round bowl of punch and his voice whimpering like a weaning pup's. And who would I be, eh? Why, I'd be the good Master What-d'ye-call-um himself, him that's head cock at the house of Mrs Brett. You won't know him, but I do: he's one that looks as if he had spoke like a Ben Jonson every time he farts! But they were close that night, those two – close as a couple of candles in a tallow-chandler's basket – and talking each of them nine words at once.'

'About what?' asked Man.

For perhaps the first time in the quarter of a century the two men had known each other, the watchman saw a strange stiffening somewhere behind Ward's kind eyes and heard a soft catch in the voice.

'Well, I couldn't say, George. I didn't hear it at all, you know. Not at all.'

Man felt more saddened than angered. Even here, in the noise of the Turk's Head tavern and with a long friend, the watchman was gently reminded of how low he stood in the city. There were so many people he could not meet, so many questions he must not ask. Ned Ward, however, was one of those who had been there – in the great houses – eating there, talking there, he had stayed as long as he liked. And now it made him different, somehow distant, with a whole new set of family secrets.

It was past nine by now, and Man was becoming visibly restless. The thief-catcher might not come.

'But how do you think the catcher might help you steer Dick Savage clear of Tyburn? He's still most of a greenhorn in this city, I'd say.' The publican freshened his mouth with a tarry bush of new tobacco.

'He knows – ' the watchman was now reluctant to say anything – 'he knows the Sinclair family somewhat closer than I do. You can guess that Mr Abraham Sinclair is hardly anxious to see me in his house after the night at Robinson's, and as yet I know the others of the family not at all. I've only just seen the last son and the youngest daughter, and those but for a moment.'

'But why should you wish to know them any better, George?' Ned Ward sounded honestly puzzled.

This was a question that Man would find almost impossible to answer. It had to do with his wanting to save the life of his young friend, Richard Savage. He could think of only one way to do it: find out as much as he could about what steps might have led to the murder, what context lay about it. The first seemed to point to William Merchant; the second, to the oddly ingrown Sinclair family. But now time was against him; he needed help.

With a lurch the poet-publican brought his black breath closer to the watchman to give him the benefit of his deep experience. 'If you'd be taught by me, George, you'd turn your steps back towards Ironmonger Row and leave Soho Square to itself in your rear. Ned Ward buys his Canary from that house in Beer Lane, and he knows a little more than he'd like about that Old Nick and his damned brood. They always say there's no harm done when a good child's got, but to my mind most of the seed that Father Sinclair has raised has been cursed with rather too much loving than too little. You know of the other son that was killed in the Park, don't you, George? I thought you would. But did you know that the one girl, Philippa, has since that day kept to her dark room and in her blackest clothes in loving remembering of him? And is it true that she calls herself "Widow", even to her own father's face?' Ned Ward snorted and showed Man a permanently streaked palm. 'But on that one, Sir, I say no more.

'And the older sister, Hester, is another. A hard woman – hard as the upper leather on a drayman's shoe, cold as a cricket in an ice-house. I saw her once myself at the house: an emptied-out maid with a mole on her nose the size of Old Tom, her clothes hung on according to the Drury Lane mode, and a close smell in the corners of her as bad as a Southwark ditch or a tanner's yard in August. And do you know what it is about her, then?' The old publican dropped his voice to a juicy hush. 'I think myself there stands an agreement betwixt herself and her father: she keeps to her bed and he, George – keeps to hers!'

'And the remaining son, Walter?' Man asked him casually.

Ward snicked his lips in disappointment. 'No, Sir, not that one. Mad as May-butter is little Walter. He counts for less than nothing.'

'Even at the trade?'

'I didn't say that, now,' the other answered cautiously, eyeing the watchman. 'You'll want to remember this, George: If ever you see a lawyer whipped for lying – or a madman hanged for speaking of truth – then I'll be bound myself to prove my wig a rolling wheelbarrow!' And he solemnly and mysteriously raised both hands to twist a pair of invisible handles at his temples.

Ned Ward would probably have gone on to say more, but his drawer came over to confer with him, and the next minutes were devoted to a detailed discussion of punch in shop terms that Man could scarcely recognize. The watchman politely shifted himself sideways on his chair and idly checked the room.

The tavern had entered one of those sedate moments that come at times inexplicably to all haphazard groupings. The far corners of the room had emptied and darkened, a smoky hush fell over tired friends, at some tables men sat horribly alone. The card-playing soldiers were feeling the dry-mouthed sourness of passing drunkenness, all but one grumbling thickly over his stale luck. The majority of the churchmen were dozing, their dead pipes hanging in a pout from their slackened lips. Even the eternal conversation of gathered cups seemed to have receded into the distance as if they were being quietly stored away in another shop, in another street.

Man turned back to find his friend looking at him in a curious way – measuring him, weighing him, as one man examines another before a fight. Then the publican's old eyes lost their focus and went blank, and Man felt as though he had been gently asked to step back.

The watchman set both forearms upon the table and leant forward.

'I'll ask you only one thing more, Ned. Now this same year there have been missed from the warehouse in Beer Lane enough wares to—'

'Not missed, child,' Ward broke in, 'never missed. Merely steered down a different street towards a better buyer.'

Man showed all the surprise he did not feel.

'By whose hand, then? James Sinclair's?'

A pair of furrows in Ned Ward's grainy forehead disappeared beneath the orange handkerchief.

'Whose else's, man? He wanted all the running of the business for himself, didn't he? Wasn't the son a vessel of the same clay, a chip of the same old block, as the father?'

'But could Abraham Sinclair himself have known aught of it, do you think?' asked Man.

For the second time in less than an hour, Man thought, my old friend is going to shut me out, give me the answer that is no answer. He had seen the eyelids flicker shyly, almost like a reddening girl's, and he had heard the voice trying to swallow itself.

But then Ned Ward growled a laugh. 'But who can say? What man but the King himself knows which hip his sweet Queen takes her sleep on? And there are more gods in this city, George, than the King alone, and what they do the like of us can't guess at.'

He carefully clawed the tobacco dripping from his cheek and deposited it upon a corner of the table.

'Mr Abraham Sinclair,' he went on moodily, more to himself than to the watchman, 'is a sinful, raving, merciless old devil. Have you seen what hangs there at the ends of his arms? Talons, George, not hands. Talons to take and hold and never let go. If you want my thought, it is he that should have died how many years back in the stead of his devil of a brother that was burned to cold ashes in the house in Soho Square!' Ned Ward shook his head fiercely, then nodded across the table at Man. 'No, George. I think if the father had known what his son was at, you'd have found the marks of his fangs in his throat, and the old man could still be heard gargling the blood.'

They kept a long silence between them, the publican poking at his bolus of tobacco, until Man asked: 'Do you know anything more of the dead brother?'

Suddenly Ned Ward sat up and brightened as a long shadow divided the table. 'No time now, George. Here's your man. Ah, Henry! You'll sit and share some punch with us, won't you?'

The handsome face of the thief-catcher, Henry Fielding, spread in an honest smile. 'No man need dread a return to dust, Ned, that daily wets his clay!'

Fielding fitted his tall frame at the table and glanced from man to man.

'I wonder now if either of you would know of any work to be got for a simple boy from the country?'

Chapter 15

Kitty had been here too many times before – both to visit and to stay – yet she had never been able to get used to it. It was the cold of Newgate Prison that hurt her most, a cold of inert stones and inert lives, a cold of chilling hopelessness. It worked itself into her bones until nothing could warm them. For some others, she knew, the prison could be a place of shelter or entertainment or even trade; for her, it was only the horrid antechamber leading to the jungles of America or to the triple-headed gallows at Tyburn.

She had been here last on Monday, the twenty-fourth of May, 1725, to witness the last moments of her one-time master, Jonathan Wild. She had brought him a pot of laudanum and helped to steady it in his shaking hand. She had served him in other ways, too, and the iron cold on her bared skin had stayed rooted in her chest for weeks afterward. And now, as she walked numbly through the hopeless rooms of Newgate Prison, she could feel it clogging her lungs again. Nothing had changed.

A kind man whose face hung in tatters of scar tissue took her to a less crowded corner where the stones in the ancient walls were sweating a black damp. She found the street-porter, William Merchant, squatting upon a patch of grey straw and trying to warm his face at an emaciated candle. The light lifted his features up into a satanic leer. He looked ridiculously, dangerously happy.

Another, bigger man lay curled into a comma off to one side, sleeping. Kitty knew him, too. James Gregory.

The squatting man, suddenly irritated, sat back to look up at her.

'What's the day?'

'The twenty-third of the month, Bill.'

'The day, slut! The day!'

125

'Oh. Why, it's Thursday.'

The street-porter pondered for a moment.

'You're early, then.'

'But only by a few days, Bill,' Kitty pleaded. 'And I do so need the money quick, you know. And I did bring them all into where you said and when—'

'Quiet, can't you!'

He looked fearfully at his sleeping companion, waited to hear the regular breathing, then dropped his voice to a hoarse panting.

'But I've not got it here, Kitty, you see. Not yet. I'll need someone to run out to get what's due me, before I can give any to you.'

The woman slid back an inch, and her shoulders sagged unevenly. She did not want to say what he expected her to say, but the stones of the prison felt so cold.

'Well, Bill, I think I've always tried to do the best I could for you. I–I could go for you, if you've no one else.'

'That's my Kitty!' He squatted forward again. 'Now do you know where is the Brett house? You do? So run yourself off to there tomorrow early and ask out the steward of the place. Name of Peters. Straight man, looks like he's holding a fishbone up his arse. Tell him you're from me, and tell him my work's been done.' He glanced quickly at James Gregory. 'The man's here. The rest is theirs.'

Kitty was worried. 'And will he give me it?'

'He'll give it, he'll give it. Just do what I tell you.' He brought the candle closer to his sharp eyes. 'And you see, girl, that every farthing of it's brought back to me here. Or there's no place for you far enough away from me.'

'Oh, Bill . . .'

'And see you get yourself ready for the trial. You're into it now; you can't get out.'

Then he blew the candle out with a hiss, and Kitty was suddenly wrapped in the kind of darkness only the blind can know, waking from a yearning dream of day.

It took her a long time to make her way out of Newgate Prison. There were so many turnings, so many rooms that opened only into other, darker rooms. A man – or a woman – could waste the rest of his life in trying to get out. Coming finally out into the breathing street was like being born again.

Kitty was a hard girl; yet now, as she hurried towards her room in Westminster, she was scared. But not for herself. Now she was frightened for a young man – a gentleman – a man she had seen only once, a man she did not even know.

And in Soho Square another man – younger, about Kitty's own age – stood in the front hallway of a large house and strained to hear something through a closed door. He tried to listen with his whole body – with the pale fingertips pressed weakly against the wood, the boy's face furrowed in concentration, the delicate back arched into attention. He was listening for a cough, a sigh, the merest crinkling of a paper – anything to tell him what the man inside the room was doing. What was he thinking? What was he planning? Would he sometimes call out for him? The young man yearned bodily towards the door. Or had he forgotten completely that he was in the house?

Walter Sinclair was alone in the front hallway; he might as well have been alone in the house. This house had always felt too big for him. It had too many rooms, too many halls and turnings, too many doors and windows – and all of them were always closed and bolted. There was no way out. And only one man had the keys – the cold, old man with the night-black eyes who now sat working alone in his room while his last son stood shivering with love and unhappiness outside the door.

The young man could not breathe. He padded softly away towards the front door, found it locked, then turned gasping to move towards the back of the house. As he passed the door to his father's workroom, he unconsciously swerved slightly to brush his shoulder against the frame; then he almost ran down the hallway, hiccuping for air, terrified at his own mad boldness.

At the rear of the hall stood a useless alcove which Walter Sinclair liked to think of as his own. He had spent many hours sheltering there, when he was sure the rest of the house would not miss him. No one could disturb him there, nothing could reach him – except for the dreaded thunder of his father's voice in anger.

Now the young man laid the back of his head against the wall and tried to pull the air into his lungs. It calmed him somewhat, and he began to pick spastically at the material of his shirt. This calmed him, too. But then he began to wonder if the minute puff of the torn lint might not reach his father's ears, if his cowering here might not be seen. The old man was everywhere. The members of the family were his arms and legs; he could feel every twitch, every thought. Was that impossible?

Walter Sinclair whimpered to himself. He had to get out. Somehow. But who would help him? Not his mother, no. Not Hester. She was the father's – what? Not Philippa. She was too busy with her strange grief. Sophia, then? Sophia had always been kind to him, kinder than the others, though impatient. And maybe she, too, would want to escape – now.

The sharp iron echo of a latch and the workroom door was opened and closed and his father's footsteps coming towards him down the hall and Walter tried frantically to merge himself with the wall behind him. Then Abraham Sinclair, ignoring all shadows, turned to pass through the door into his head-steward's room.

In his alcove Walter Sinclair clenched his small fists white. Who strikes first, strikes best.

Sophia, he thought. *Sophia*.

Chapter 16

The odd thing was that Man had once arrested Henry Fielding's father, and now it helped to create something of a bond between them. There was another thing, too, although Man did not like to think of it: the young thief-catcher was the same age as George and Sarah's own son would be – if he were still with them.

It had taken his first sight of Henry Fielding's distinctively handsome face to nudge the watchman's memory. He had remembered back to 1716. Man and another watchman had been called to one of the most notorious gaming-houses in the City and had found Edmund Fielding – drunk, proud, and roaring – holding his own against a pack of snarling gamesters. Man had arrested him on the scene, charging him with playing the illegal game of faro, but it was only a ploy for getting him safely out of the room. His opponents had spotted certain irregularities in Edmund Fielding's handling of the cards, and they had been anxious to discuss it with him at length. Once outside, Man had steered the weaving squire towards the nearest coaching-inn and wished him a safe journey back to Dorset.

Henry Fielding had all the robust swagger of his father, but he wore it better. In him it was the breathless exuberance of a healthy man at the opening of his adult life who saw laid out before him all the numberless possibilities of a long and active life. He could make of himself what he would. He had a family behind him that was well, yet not lethargically settled; he was newly come from Eton College with the indispensable background in the classics; he was an unusually tall and attractive man, ruggedly built, with a clean energy that was cheering to see. Hopeful and confident, he could outlaugh anybody; yet the next moment, hearing of someone else's trouble, he would be as sober and caring as a country vicar. There was a basic, though rough humanity in him that deserved Man's respect at their very first meeting.

The year before, Henry Fielding had come up to London for the first time and found himself running through the more reckless streets. It was mostly unavoidable. He was new to the town, a country boy hungering for adventure, with no clear idea of what might lie before him. He had thrown himself thoughtlessly into anything that came his way. The watchman guessed, too, that Fielding might have been fleeing some recent disappointment in love. Once, when Man had mentioned his own wife by name, he had seen the clear, frank face cloud with anguish, and the young man had quickly changed the topic.

In the middle of 1726, Henry Fielding had suddenly set himself up as a professional thief-catcher. Man wondered what had made him think of choosing such a disreputable occupation.

'Almost the first name I heard spoken in London,' he told the watchman during their first talk at Ned Ward's, 'even before the King's, was that of Jonathan Wild. I took to studying the published records of his life, especially those by Defoe and Captain Alexander Smith. I thought that any man whose name could live so loudly in the streets, even after his death, must have been a man of peculiar talents. I myself, Sir, do not wish my own name never to be remembered.'

Man asked him if he wanted, then, to end his career as Mr Wild had his, and the thief-catcher became instantly more serious.

'No, Sir, it is not that. It is only that I think the office can be made to work both honestly and honourably, if it is held by the right sort of man. And the people will welcome it – I believe this – even more gladly than they welcomed Mr Wild's vicious, un-natural reign. The man caused more thievery than he cured, and all men knew it.'

'And abetted it, because it meant more weight in their own pockets.'

'True,' Fielding conceded, looking at first disheartened. 'But what is the end of it? The people lose their native respect for their laws, for their neighbours, and finally for themselves. And at last, I think, they begin to weary of the animal savagery in their streets

– the beatings waiting for them in every dark lane, the rapes promised their wives and daughters in any lonely alley, the emptying of their homes while they sleep. You know all this better than I, Mr Man, from your former work. And you know the many magistrates and judges, with all their snivelling myrmidons, who are very little better than the foulest bully in Golden Lane. Our own true Mr Justice Page is one. Since ascending to the King's Bench in September, he has shown us all the shadow of his hand. He would hang a man for sneezing in his coat, yet be the first to sell a Tyburn Ticket at the nearest corner.'

'Is it so much better in your own country?' Man asked him.

'None better, Sir, none better. But as the wen runs, so it infects the rest of the body. What is needed first, Sir, is an ordering within the town, before we can begin any ordering without.'

Man was as impressed by the gravity of the young thief-catcher's intelligence as he was charmed by his essential goodness and his raw humour. After Man had accompanied him to his rooms at Little Turnstile and the two had settled themselves over cups and pipes, the watchman asked him if he meant to be always satisfied with the questionable fame of his present office. After a moment, Fielding went to burrow in a desk drawer and came back with a small square of paper.

'For the time when I achieve some worthier renown.'

Man read the ornately written script:

This is to give notice to all the world, and especially to all and any men who were wilfully ignorant of the personal qualities of the undersigned during his obscure days, that the discovered a–e of same shall be laid open to their bussing at his home during the hours of his rest. Witness my hand, Henry Fielding.

And there was no telling which Man laughed at harder, the audacious advertisement itself or the sheepish expression on the young man's face as he returned the paper to the drawer.

As delightful as the notice was, it gave the watchman a pretext for opening the subject that was uppermost in his mind: the inexplicable murder of James Sinclair and the desperate situation of the young poet, Richard Savage. Man soon learned that Fielding already knew as much of the incident as could be gleaned from Ned Ward and from the streets, and he was eager enough to tell him the rest.

'So Count Ugly himself was present, was he?'

Man bitterly related the history of his own troubles with John James Heidegger.

'What you need do, Sir, is only to tease the Swiss into some position from which he must look to you to save himself from shame. He now depends much upon the good humour of the town. Threaten him with the loss of that, and you have him.' Fielding considered for a moment. 'Or, if all else fails you, you might tuck the toe of your boot into that place on him where the two meet the one and have done with it – though this is a country remedy and may not answer here.'

'No,' Man said, smiling, 'we use it much here in the town, too.'

Man tried to give Henry Fielding some notion of his own misgivings about the underlying causes of the murder. He assured him that he wanted only to find some way of lessening the severity of Richard Savage's punishment, and learning more about the victim's family and business seemed to be the only road open to him. It was here that Fielding could help him, if he would. The street-porters, William Merchant and James Gregory, Man was saving for himself.

'And the girl, Kitty?'

'I think she lies outside of this,' Man answered. 'Only another feature of the streets, nothing more.'

'Yet it was she that took you all to Robinson's.'

Man said nothing.

The thief-catcher had seen Richard Savage a few times, but never met him. Yet he knew the man's history, his pathetic series of misfortunes, and he seemed ready to help. And there was nothing, apparently, that he knew better in London than the complicated family of Abraham Sinclair.

'They are altogether too much like a single body, that crew. The father is the head, of course, as he should be; but the wife and children, that ought to be the arms and legs of him, appear more like the raw guts that cannot be let out except through death. They bleed and they function, but the doing so only twists them up amongst themselves. Here, I can give you an instance of what I mean.

'I can't say exactly what Abraham Sinclair may have thought fit to tell you, but I am sure he would not have told you all. You should know, then, that there have been this year several large subtractions of material from the company's house in Beer Lane – losses which the father neither authorized nor knew aught of. Or so he said to me. At any rate, it was what first moved him to hire me. The work proved to be transparent enough. In a few weeks I was able to determine that the son – this James that has just died – along with his sister, Sophia, was directing the goods into hidden hands at his own pleasure. I saw it mainly as an effort to usurp the trade from the father who, as you know, is too old now to steer it aright himself. It is, I fear, the natural desire of all sons.'

The thief-catcher seemed to wonder how to continue.

'I told Mr Sinclair all. I question now if I should have done so, but I think a man is obliged, both by his God and his own conscience, to discover the truth he knows. What troubled me at the time – and troubles me still, Sir – is that the father seemed to know as much of the affair as myself. Or more. If I knew mankind something better than I do, I could swear I thought him pleased at the news. It was this that I meant when I said that the family were his inside. He wore the grin of the mad valetudinarian whose medico has at last found the ulcer in his bowels that he has been complaining of all his days.'

As delicately as he could, Man asked him: 'And did you tell him also of the girl's part in it?'

'I . . . did not, Sir. I don't think a man should knowingly betray the woman he – admires. I did tell her, though. I thought she might want to free herself from such a shameful business before it came too late.'

'And what was her response?'

Fielding suddenly seemed to feel an unevenness in the seat of his chair.

'She called me a puppy.'

He said it so quietly – then paused for a time – then lifted his head with a shake.

'That is one dame, Sir, that is entirely too much man for me!'

The watchman did not want to press him. He knew what it was to love a woman who could not accept any degree of gentleness in a man. They wanted it, until they had it.

'Philip Sidney knew of it,' Man said helpfully. '—"Is constant love deemed there but want of wit?" It is the price we sometimes have to pay, Sir.'

Now it was Man's turn to tell Henry Fielding something he did not know. The watchman described for him the killing of Jacob Sinclair four years ago in St James's Park. When he had finished, he waited for the thief-catcher to work it out for himself.

Finally, Fielding looked as shocked as the watchman had expected him to be.

'They're all but the same, then!'

Man nodded. 'Just that. It is not every family that loses two of its sons to the violence of total strangers. Two brothers – both unknown to their murderers, both attacked without reason, both baited to their separate deaths. I can accept the first, Sir – we have all of us seen stranger sights – but I cannot accept the second.'

Henry Fielding said something about the tyranny of coincidence, but the watchman would have none of it.

'There is this, though,' he added. 'Jacob Sinclair met his death at the hands of a soldier – one William Hawksworth – who was afterwards hanged for his troubles. Now I have learned that this same Hawksworth had once worked for the Sinclair business and that he was roughly removed from it by order of the father himself. So that even if he did not know the son, Jacob – who kept himself mostly distant from the work in Beer Lane – he would still have known Abraham Sinclair, and he would have had true enough cause to hate him. And with the father standing out of reach, what better vengeance could he find than to attack the son?'

The other found an objection. 'Yet your friend Savage has told you that he knew nothing of either the family or the business. He could have no reason, then, to grudge against the father or to wreak his malice against the son.'

'But could it be that the other man, William Merchant, has? Or might there be some hidden connection between Savage and the Sinclair family, something even he himself cannot know, that would make of him the properest tool for the deed? It is here that I need you, Sir: to penetrate into the family in my stead.'

'Through which doorway, then?'

'Is there any other open to you,' Man said gently, 'but Sophia?'

It took Man a long time, over an hour, to overcome the thief-catcher's objections. Most of these had to do with a young man's normal feelings of shame and resentment against the woman who has rejected him. The watchman had expected these. And there was the lasting disappointment that Fielding did not try to hide, saying that 'He had never known a woman that had such worthiness in her, but that it was sleeping.' Yet beyond all this was something more.

'That house in Soho Square has its own air about it. It is the air of a room in which some man has lain dying a very long time. You've been there yourself, Sir; you must have felt it. Inside is a smothering closeness, a dead cold that has nothing of the clean, bracing cold of the country in winter. The one can quicken; the other, only leaden. And it is too hidden within itself, like a man's worst thoughts. Nothing can come in, nothing can go out; and if there is any love in the place, it's the self-love of the crazed animal that is trapped and starving and forced to feed upon itself. I'll help you help your friend, if I can; but I will not welcome a return to that house or its family. It stinks of fear – as much as a tallow chandler's melting-room, as our friend Mr Ward would say.'

Before he left Fielding's rooms, Man knew that he had to settle the matter of the fee. The thief-catcher was a shrewd young man. With the guilt or innocence of Richard Savage still so undecided, he said, he would be unwise to give of himself for nothing. The watchman had nothing to give; but luckily he had learned that Fielding had a play in hand that he was anxious to have performed. The young man's second cousin, the Lady Mary Wortley Montagu, could help him some, but he needed a closer contact with the working theatre. Man had only to mention two of Savage's closest friends and steadiest benefactors – the actress, Anne Oldfield, and the co-manager of the Theatre Royal, Robert Wilks – and the joy they would both feel at the Bastard's release, and in a minute the deal was closed.

For the next two weeks, the two men worked together, though apart, to try to save the life of the luckless Richard Savage. Every two or three days, they would meet at Little Turnstile to match cups of ale and trade information. Henry Fielding was a mighty drinker: more than once the watchman mistook his way back to Ironmonger Row. And as the day of the trial drew nearer, both men started to spend more of the evening with their ale than with their news. They had little enough to show for their efforts, and now they had less and less time left them.

For all his dislike of the Sinclair family, the young thief-catcher seemed to take to the work. Man suspected that he was happy just to be in Sophia's company again, however much it might have cost his pride. Fielding had at first presented himself at the family warehouse to offer his sympathy to the dead man's sister, and now he went there daily to talk and to take dinner with her in the neighbourhood. The girl seemed strangely glad to see him again. Since her brother's death, she had been staying at the warehouse all day with her remaining brother Walter in order to keep the trade moving smoothly. And as the last Sinclair son stood useless and befuddled in the middle of the whirling floor, Sophia Sinclair would keep Fielding out of bounds, chattering freely with the tips of her fingers resting comfortably upon his arm, as if he were precisely the man she had been waiting for all her life. The thief-catcher told Man that what worried him most was this change in the girl: 'I should sooner expect to find the sun lying among my folded stockings!'

But Fielding learned little. Sophia Sinclair did not know Richard Savage. No one, she swore, either in the Sinclair household or at the warehouse, knew anything of him, of his supposed family, of any of his friends. She was completely certain of this. She agreed that her brother Jacob had probably been killed four years earlier out of the soldier's spite against her father; but that was missing in the death of James, which seemed to her nothing more than the result of a meaningless brawl. How could it have been anything other than accident, when even James himself had been a stranger to his murderer?

Man shook his head. 'You should have told her that, at the very moment of the attack, her brother gave a cry of recognition that was meant for Savage and no one else.'

Fielding began sweating in the chilly room at Little Turnstile and averted his face from the watchman's.

'I did that. She had her answer ready.'

'What was it?'

'Well,' the thief-catcher stammered, 'she said that her brother must have cried out more in surprise than in anything else. A – surprise that his attacker was different from the man he had been long expecting.'

Man considered it. 'It's possible – just. He may have been holding himself ready for a charge from another direction and at the instant of his death simply could not explain away the new-comer. Yes, I can see it. Who was it he was most in fear of, then?'

'Who?' Fielding nervously wet his lips and tried to smile. 'Well, she said – *she* said, do you mind me? – ah, that it was you.'

The pipe dropped from Man's mouth. 'Sir!'

'I cannot help it, George! 'Tis what the girl herself said, plain as a pack-saddle!'

'But what by the eyes of God can it mean?'

The thief-catcher was quick to say he didn't know, that Sophia Sinclair could not give the reason for it. But she promised it was true, having heard it darkly hinted by her brother even on the day of his death, and Man and Fielding had to be content in believing what they had no chance to understand.

Walter Sinclair was a separate mystery. Fielding spent much of his time watching him and a little of it talking with him. He found him greatly changed from a few months ago – more deeply nervous, even more wide in the mind, with a wholly new battery of spasms and uncertainties in his look. Fielding had no desire to be unkind, but he thought the boy was stark raving mad.

'What would you call him, George, who daily riddles you a riddle about how Craven shall not cry craven until he be dead and gone once for always?'

'What is it, then, this Craven? A name?'

Fielding sat back. 'Well, it is. It's his that burned himself to death long before Walter Sinclair was born. Craven's the name of Abraham's brother. I call this rank lunacy, Sir, don't you?'

Man looked grim and thoughtful, but said nothing.

For his part, the watchman felt during these two weeks as if he had been doomed to wander forever in one place. He did what he could. Most of one day was passed in the cold despair of Newgate Prison, trying to extract some information from any one of the three prisoners. But for all that he was able to learn from them, Man might as well have stayed warm and resting at home.

Richard Savage was no help at all. He was among friends, but they were chilling him to the heart. With his young face become dispirited and stupid, he was willing to talk of nothing but the special suit of clothes he had ordered from his best tailor in which he meant to die. That, and the hopeless plea of self-defence which Man knew could not be made to work, were the Bastard's only thoughts. Man stayed with him for over an hour and spoke no more than a dozen words. When the watchman stood up, Savage roused himself enough to ask his friend finally to discharge his costly rooms in Westminster. He would not, he said with a loose laugh, be needing them any more. Man said he would see to it at once.

The street-porter, James Gregory, surprised Man with his brooding silence. The watchman had expected better of the honest young countryman. Instead, he sat as stunned and uncomprehending as a wired hare. Man tried to get him to talk of that night in Robinson's Coffee-House, but the porter would say nothing more than that it was all an accident, a sad accident. To Man, he seemed distant and worried, oddly evasive, almost protective; but the watchman could not believe him guilty of anything – except perhaps of innocence.

From William Merchant, Man could get nothing but curses.

'Go back to your proud gentleman that got me in here, will

you? Tell him I think him a son of a bitch and that I damn his poxed eyes!'

Outside the prison Man fared even worse. The girl, Kitty, was not to be found; and Man wondered where she could have got the money to forsake her usual work in the night streets. Neither Savage's mother nor her head steward would condescend to being interviewed by a lowly watchman. And the owner of the rooms in Westminster – a perpetually drunken man with yellowed skin and a smell of stale urine – gloomily traded Savage's few clothes and papers for Man's money, saying that the last time he had sent a letter to Richmond was to wish the new King and Queen his best.

On Wednesday night, 6 December, the watchman and Fielding sat long together over their emptying cups and their baking pipes. They had exchanged whatever scanty information they had – reviewed it, discussed it, all but turned it inside out. The thief-catcher wanted to move on at once to the house in Soho Square. He wanted to question the servants, the children – especially the father – in order to understand the obscure workings of the Sinclair family. He had never met anything to compare with it, he said, in the country. Man thought he had all the ambitious curiosity of the doctor confronted with a new and wasting disease.

The watchman was for holding back and trusting, as he always had, to the living resources of the street. He was waiting for something, looking for the smallest detail, that would help him find the surrounding context for all that had happened. And it was also true that, although he would never admit as much to young Henry Fielding, he could not yet endure the thought of facing again the insupportable eyes of Abraham Sinclair.

There was one thing the two men did agree upon.

It was slow work. It would take a lot of time.

And tomorrow was the day of the trial.

Chapter 17

Man came a few minutes late to the Old Bailey and as a result soon found himself seated next to one of the most notorious men in all England.

He recognized him at once, though the two had never met. It would be hard to mistake the man whom some Grub Street wits, despising his religion, had already dubbed 'Pope Alexander'. He sat like a folded grasshopper upon a mound of borrowed coats, and even then a space in front had had to be cleared for him to see. Man judged him to be no more than four and a half feet tall; yet the gross ledge of the humpback, the knob of the chest, and the twigs of the limbs made him seem smaller and frailer than any grown man could be – an exaggerated child. He was dressed well, but with enough clothes for three, though the hall was baking with the crowd. A spattered inkhorn wavered impossibly upon his knee, as he worked intently to cover a sheet with a scratching, almost indecipherable handwriting.

Man liked his face best of all: the keen profile was as lovely as a girl's, but matured by the lines at the mouth, the corded muscles in the cheek, the headache contractions above the eyebrows. The watchman knew he was a decade older than his neighbour, yet he did not dare to greet him with anything more than an abbreviated bow.

Reviewing the restless, excited hall, Man was mildly surprised to see how many wealthy and distinctive persons had come to witness Savage's trial. A few the watchman knew by sight: the Lord Tyrconnel, the powerful nephew of Savage's mother; the playwright, Aaron Hill; a careful disorder of hair and hat that could only belong to the actress, Anne Oldfield. There were many more whom Man did not recognize, but he could single them out from the crowd by their dress and the way they held their heads, and by the flurries of nods and winks and smirks that inevitably surrounded them. It never failed to astound him how a man as chronically destitute as Richard Savage could have so many and such important people who called him their friend – at least when it was convenient for them to do so.

Man looked towards the three prisoners, standing uneasily in a delta before the bench. It seemed to him that Savage had regained his spirits in the last few days. He stood straighter, gazed about the hall calmly and masterfully, at times even suggested a smile. He was the focus of all eyes, and he bore it well. The watchman was proud of him.

The other two, the street-porters, did not have Savage's style. James Gregory had the look of a man who feels a constant internal pain that he cannot understand. He could show none of the confidence of his friend, William Merchant, who had the sour peevishness of a hurried man waiting for the street to clear. For some reason, Man found himself staring at him until he felt his eyes watering.

The hall was a gathered motley of sounds: ceaseless conversation without words, the snapping of exchanged snuff-boxes, the cough that is started in one corner and then relayed to the farthest ends of the room. Man was barely conscious of it – until it suddenly paused, until the hall all at once caught its breath. He did not need to look to know what it meant.

Sir Francis Page was nearing seventy now; but as he entered the hall and strode towards the bench, he left his clerks wheezing in his wake. He was not a big man – heavy with meat and beer, flushed with spite, but never torpid – yet when he came into a crowded room, he was the only one there. His eyes were small and sunken, but they missed nothing: not the slightest tremor of a frightened hand, not the most private weakness. He would never be surprised by either force or cleverness. He would never be wrong.

'In the words of the Dorchester thatcher,' Man heard suddenly from the poet beside him: ' "God, in his rage, Made a Judge Page." '

Justice Page grunted himself into his chair and dug his elbows into his papers. He looked wearily about the hall, but the only man he saw was Richard Savage.

'Your name, Sir!'

'My name is Richard Savage, your Lordship.'

'Savage, is it?' Justice Page looked at the accused almost shyly. 'Pray, then, tell us who was your father?'

The watchman had not expected such a question, but he saw his friend's shoulders square and heard his voice deepen manfully.

'I am, my Lord, the natural son to the late Earl Rivers!'

The hall produced its required murmur, but Justice Page took no notice of it.

'So you say, then, so you say...'

Man was feeling the heat of the room at the back of his neck and worrying about what would come next. He had heard some in the town say that Justice Page took a hangman's rope to bed with him each night, drawn as tightly as could be for his pleasure.

'Yet I read here in my papers, Sir, that you and your fellows have been charged in the foul death of one Mr James Sinclair, as it happened in a private room in Robinson's Coffee-House upon the twentieth of this month last. Now the Sinclair family,' Page went on smoothly, 'is known well in this town and esteemed – though not nearly so highly, of course, as is ... your own. Yet I have never heard the smallest action ever being brought against the good Mr James Sinclair, whereas you – ' fingering through his papers, but not looking – 'well, we find you, Sir, in 'fifteen brought before Mr Justice Wooleston to answer for a pair of seditious pamphlets – now I believe I have the names of them somewhere here before me ...'

Savage spoke up. 'I do not think, my Lord, that any man's youthful enthusiasms should be—'

The voice of Justice Page had the ability to double in power without becoming louder, so that even the distracted carman near the far door suddenly felt his words in his coat.

'What is your plea, Sir?'

'I am not guilty, my Lord,' Savage calmly replied with no hesitation at all, 'by reason of—'

'Yes, we shall hear that later, Sir, if it please you. First the witnesses!'

Sitting next to the still-scribbling, humpbacked poet, George Man prepared himself for a period of uneasy boredom. He foresaw no surprises in the depositions of the witnesses: none of them could have any reason to favour the accused. Yet none of them, he felt sure, would swear to anything that could not have happened. Whoever else was in the room that night must now be feeling as confused as the watchman.

Only two things troubled him greatly. First, Man had not yet been able to locate John James Heidegger among the crowd, though the Swiss Count could have been expected to commandeer the most visible chair. And then the watchman was beginning to fret and worry for himself: he knew that he would soon be called as a witness against his friend, and he had absolutely no idea how he was going to tell it.

The landlady from Robinson's Coffee-House was the first to be detached from the crowd. She came forward all nods and curtsies and studied obsequiousness, never presuming to raise her eyes to the level of the judge. Throughout her memorized account, she kept returning insistently to a single theme.

'Drunk, was he? Well, he was as far in his altitudes as any I've ever seen! Now who made him that way I don't know, but it weren't myself that done it, may't please your Worship.'

Savage flexed forward to object, but the watchman did not see him. He was looking only at William Merchant.

Justice Page rudely cut the landlady short. 'Call us your maid, will you?'

The husky girl appeared with her head extravagantly bandaged. She detailed her sufferings at some length, then displayed her wound to the twelve gentlemen of the jury even before they asked for it. Justice Page was careful not to interrupt her, until she began remembering how dark it had been and how many men with swords and how she had always *thought* it was Mr Savage that had cut her – then he tossed her aside like a fishbone picked clean.

Now it was the watchman's turn, and he had not even got to the front of the hall before he noticed the sweat starting to leak down coldly from his temples.

Man told it as well as he could. He left out nothing, but he was most cautious not to add any of the imagined embellishments that are so often attached to remembered events. Nothing could harm Savage more.

The judge let the watchman finish – almost.

'Now I am told, Sir, that Mr James Sinclair took his death in the belly. That is the truth of it, no?'

Man found himself staring at something that was hanging from the tip of Page's jagged nose.

'Well, I was down, Sir, as I have said. And from my place on the floor—'

'– you should have been able to see it better than any!' Page snarled. 'Am I right or am I wrong, Sir? Eh?'

'Yet the overturned table stood between me and the rest of the company.'

'Nah, nah, nah!' Justice Page waggled his jowls and rose reddening from his chair. 'Now, fellow, have done with your milky humming and hawing, and tell us the straight English of it! Did you or didn't you see this man Savage here give the wound? Yea or nay, Sir!'

The hall was silent, but there was a subtle hollowness sounding in the watchman's ears. He saw the advancing point of the sword, the puncturing of Sinclair's clothes, the shaft taking hours to shorten – but Man's voice was steady.

'I did not!'

Page stormed. 'Blind, man, you're blind – blind as the rest of the poxed watch in this goddamned city! Where is he, then?' he asked the hall. 'Where's the man that was with you?'

A shuffling started up behind the watchman, a wave of pardonings and shunted chairs that rolled quickly towards him. He turned his head to see the shambling figure of John James Heidegger, the Swiss Count, proudly dividing the crowd in all his ugly glory—

– only it was not John James Heidegger whom Man saw emerging from the press. It was a much younger man, a shrunken man whose body was distorted by consumption and a twisted leg. Man had never seen him before.

'Give us your name, Sir!' Page demanded.

'Robin Spiller, your Honour. I'm a gold-finder that works round Haymarket way.'

'And you were drinking and whoring with Mr James Sinclair the night he was killed at Robinson's?'

The man ducked his head shamefully. 'That was me, it was.'

'And you saw Richard Savage give the strike?'

'That I did, your Honour, clear as a maiden's water!'

The judge ignored the moment of joy this brought to the hall.

'Now tell me this, fellow: Can you recall in what posture Mr Sinclair was holding his sword when he was killed?'

'Saw it plain, your Honour – ' the small man nodded emphatically – 'and won't never forget it. The poor man was pointing his straight down to the floor, like as he wanted to show there were no more fighting in him. He'd yielded up, I could see that.'

'Yet this watchman here,' Page pressed him eagerly, 'has just told us that Mr Gregory had taken command of Mr Sinclair's sword-hand in order to stop the fight.'

The nightman kept his eyes away from Man and shrugged.

'Aye, your Honour,' he said simply. 'But that was after, don't you see – to keep it down and make it more easier.'

It went on like this for another quarter of an hour. The watchman could have objected – could have shouted that the scavenger had not been there that night, that he was only a clever substitute sent by Heidegger to preserve his reputation – but it would have changed nothing. None of the three prisoners could have noticed the Swiss Count at the time, sheltering in a dark corner with the girl, and everyone else had undoubtedly already been paid – except for Man. It was not until later that the watchman learned who Robin Spiller really was: a veteran supplier of prostitutes for Heidegger's masquerades. But now he knew the true extent of the Count's influence in the town.

Man might have had some hopes of hearing the truth from Kitty, but he lost them as soon as he saw her take her place before the bench. She looked pale and sick and scared, and all her testimony was broken by a shaking, lacerating cough. The only perfectly clear words she spoke were the most damning of all: she honestly had not seen Mr Sinclair draw his sword at all.

Justice Page, who had been mainly impressed by what he could see of Kitty's throat, asked her if she had often visited Robinson's Coffee-House.

'That house, your Worship? No, Sir, I shouldn't want myself to die in such a place!' There was a loud humph in the crowd that could be recognized as the landlady's. 'I would not have gone to there then, if I'd not been sent there.'

Back at his place in the gallery, with the crippled poet nodding off to sleep against his arm, Man wondered if he had heard her right. He stretched himself and caught her glancing towards the gloomy porter, William Merchant. She held her head down, peeking at him through the screen of her hair, like a dog begging care of a hard master. Now what woman, thought Man, ever fears a man she does not even know?

After the trio of soldiers had spent half an hour recalling that they knew nothing, Page summarized the case for the jury.

Whatever minor discrepancies might have appeared in the separate depositions, it was clear enough that Mr Merchant might have been guilty of an unjust provocation, that Mr Savage and Mr Gregory both drew their swords in outright aggression and that Mr Savage most like drew first of all, that Mr Savage did then stab Mr Sinclair without first allowing him to take a posture of defence, and that Mr Savage did thereafter endeavour to escape the rigours of the law by fleeing the scene, at the same time cutting an hurtless maid upon the head, the mark of which would subtract from her native beauty for ever and make of the remainder of her unhappy days in this life a long, unending misery.

All of this that was intended for the benefit of the gentlemen of the jury was instead directed solely towards Richard Savage. The judge cast out each phrase at the prisoner, growing more and more spiteful as he went along, like a nasty boy flicking at the nose of a caged bull with a whip. Savage stood it well; but even from where Man sat, he could see him flinch.

The trial had gone on for over three hours now, and the long gravity of it could be heard and felt in the hall. The men were grumbling for a drink and the noisy freedom of the tavern; the women were exchanging outside news and scented handkerchiefs. In every section of the hall the people were growing restless with waiting, impatient to hear Richard Savage present his defence and to witness Justice Page break out into his customary, uncontainable rage.

Just as George Man had succeeded in rousing the man at his side and drying the snake of saliva from his sleeve, Justice Page began a brief questioning of the first street-porter, James Gregory.

Had he known Mr Savage long?

'No, Sir, not at all. Only through Bill. That's Mr Merchant there.'

Were the two of them, then, such fast friends?

'Why, I can't say, Sir. Only through some business that lay between them, I think.'

What sort of business?

'I don't know.' But the simple countryman said it as if he did.

And how did he and Mr Merchant come to meet Mr Savage on the night of the twentieth?

'Well, the two of us – Bill and me – we were down together round the Sanctuaries; and after waiting for a time – well, we found him in the street and come up to him.'

Then the three of them commenced to drinking more than a good man should, wasn't that the way of it? And Mr Savage more than any?

James Gregory examined the floor at his feet.

'As to that, Sir, I don't know that I can say. But I can tell you that Bill himself was good enough to pay for every cup – and as soon as he'd ordered it, too!'

Now what was the meaning of his taking Mr Sinclair's sword-hand from him during the fight? To make him ready for the kill, wasn't it? So it was a case of three men against the one, about as womanish a trick as the judge had ever heard of.

'No, your Honour, I swear to Christ! We was only trying to stop it – the two of us, me and Bill. He had a hold of Mr Savage, and he cried me to the other. I tried – ' he shook his big fists in front of him – 'I tried to Jesus to pull him out and away from it, and Bill's pushing into t'other, and then Savage's coming right into us and there's no way and no time to slip aside of it! It was all done, your Honour, before I knew!'

Justice Page made a smooth transition to the other porter, while Man leaned forward in his chair.

Had Mr Merchant never met Mr Sinclair before?

'Never.'

Nor his father?

'Whose?'

Mr Sinclair's, of course! Had the accused still his fifteen wits about him, or what?

'And when would a fellow such as me have the chance to meet the black-eyed devil? When I took the length of his foot, eh?'

Everyone recognized this as a slur against Savage's shameful apprenticeship as a boy to a Holborn shoemaker, but Justice Page was quick to snuff out the sparks of tittering with a magisterial glare. He obviously was not about to waste any more of his time on somebody as small as William Merchant.

The last question the judge asked him was the one that Man himself would have liked to ask.

Why had Mr Merchant entered a room that was not his own and deliberately incited a brawl with a stranger that he himself could not conclude, being without arms?

And the answer was not long in coming.

'That's said simple enough,' the porter sneered, then gestured viciously towards Savage. 'It's because this damned sot of a gentleman's bastard told me to!'

Chapter 18

Neither the judge's frustrated stamping of his feet nor Richard Savage's hoarsely shouted denials could calm the mob after the street-porter's announcement. From his vantage point in the midst of it, the watchman looked around him in despair. He saw those whom he knew supported Savage turning wordless to their neighbours in blank shock, miming in disbelief, and he saw those who were against him nudging one another lewdly and grinning like apes. Some men rose half way to their feet, others rocked their heads between their hands. A covey of ladies screamed, a pair near the wall tried to faint, and a mother forgot completely about the baby she was feeding and let the breast flip dripping out of its gaping mouth. In one way or another, the whole hall registered the awful tremor of the accusation.

Justice Page was quick to take advantage of it.

'Well, Mr Richard Savage, Sir! Have you any answer to these black acts that have been laid against you? You would do well, I can tell you, to argue better for yourself than the fellow I had before me once on the country circuit that had the luck to find a horse that was not his own. He soon enough found the halter I had promised him as well!'

Savage waited out the required spasms of laughter.

'How can I respond, my Lord, to Mr Merchant's charge except to swear it is untrue? The fact that Mr Sinclair was so entirely unknown to me must show that I could not have premeditated any malice towards him or—'

'Two months was not enough for you, Sirrah?'

Savage looked lost. 'My Lord?'

'The advertisement, man!' Page bellowed, holding out a limp news-sheet. 'Your advertisement of October that named

Mr James Sinclair's murder to the day!'

'But it was not from my hand.'

'Then from whose was it? You are a poet, are you not? Ten years ago you were liberal enough with your pen, weren't you?'

'My Lord,' Savage stammered, 'I promise you I am not—'

'Or do you mean to tell us you are Mr Partridge himself, come back from hell to bubble us all? Or are you the Devil, perhaps, and fell upon Mr Sinclair only to gain his soul?'

'I meant only to say, my Lord, that however they may appear to us now, my actions in the room that night were so wholly inconsiderate and sudden that no man—'

Page tossed the sheet aside and looked sternly down at him.

'Aye, it's that way, is it? Go through it quick before the other fellow takes his chance to stand and fight.'

'My Lord, you mistake my meaning.'

'And how much better for him,' Page crowed lustily, 'if he be a natural son to the late Earl Rivers!'

It went on this way for the better part of an hour. For every point taken up by Savage on his behalf – and he argued his case gravely and intelligently – Justice Page was ready with a disruptive, bullying objection. The constant baiting gradually began to wear away at Savage. He still spoke well, even boldly, and the crowd showed its appreciation by keeping silent and still. But it was clear to all that the defence rapidly degenerated into a bitter duel between a talented nobleman, desperate for his life, and a jealous magistrate who enjoyed feeling the heft of his power in his hand. At one point, the poet sitting next to Man whispered in a breath of potted lampreys: 'It is said also of my Lord Page that he endeavours to convict only that he might savour the exquisite luxury of condemning. I think it time we feared the worst.'

Savage tried his best to establish the good characters of all three prisoners, relying mainly upon the associations of family, although he was forced to admit that he knew nothing of Mr Merchant's. He worked even harder to undermine the strength of the accusing witnesses. The watchman even had to sit and listen to his friend gently rebuke him for his having fallen to the floor and his slowness in acting. Man could only agree.

The defendant came at last to his special plea.

'And I should beg your Lordship to know that if I now propose to speak of my case *se defendendo*, it is only because—'

'How, Sir, how!' thundered Justice Page. 'Now none of your high-stomached linguo that none of these good folk here-gathered can understand. What! Are you a fugitive from the Inns of Court as well, then?'

Savage held himself in check. 'I meant only, my Lord, to allude to the certain hazard of my own life, if I had lost that opportunity of giving the thrust. Neither reason nor law, I think, obliges a man to wait—'

'You are telling us, Sir, that your life weighs more in significance than that of Mr Sinclair?'

'Of course not, my Lord.'

'Nay, Sir, but I agree!' Page grinned at the crowd. 'And we'll weigh him soon enough upon some wooden scales at Tyburn where the heavier the meat, the less the cost!'

Too many people, Man thought, cackled too gleefully at this latest gibe. The climate of the hall was subtly changing.

Savage pushed on. 'And if a man should first suffer the blow against him, he might not live to repay it. Is it not always allowable, my Lord, to prevent an assault—'

'– by lawful means, aye!'

'– and to preserve one's own life at any cost, even to the taking away of that of the adversary by whom it is endangered?'

'*If* it be endangered, Sir!'

Savage desperately raised his voice. 'Read me the law, my Lord, that inhibits a man from defending himself in whatever manner from an unprovoked attack!'

Suddenly Justice Page shot to his feet.

'Now you have said the exact words of Mr James Sinclair himself, Sirrah, could he be alive still to speak them!' He buried his fists among his papers. 'The filial son of one of this city's most renowned traders – in company with a cripple, a girl, and a drunken, fallen watchman – is surprised at his rest by a pair of mad bastards and a stupid country tout, two of them flashing their swords against him. He is then cruelly stabbed to death by the one, while the other holds him back, and his body is stripped of its goods in the dark before the felons fly for their lives. What do we call this, then, if not a murder most plain and vicious?'

'If I fled, my Lord,' Savage struggled to explain, 'it was only to avoid the long expenses and the hard severities of a gaol. I can little afford either.'

For no apparent reason, this pushed the judge into a worse frenzy of rage.

'How, fellow! Have your limbs then been so weighted down with the chains this two weeks? Have you wanted for any one thing in your chambers in Newgate? Can't I hear more guineas jingling in your gentleman's pockets even than in mine own? Why, the Ordinary writes me that even the mother you have been pleased to damn so loudly has sent you a daily pittance! Can you tell me what more any natural son to the late Earl Rivers could have the pretension to expect?'

This final bit of information surprised almost everyone in the hall, but the watchman thought that the most astonished look belonged to the street-porter, William Merchant.

There followed something of a lull in the proceedings, during which several persons of distinction stepped forward to speak for the character of the accused. The lower orders saw this as their chance to pass among themselves hard bread and cheese and short, opaque bottles. Even Man got up from his place and picked his way towards the side of the room. He already knew his friend's worth better than any; and as the trial was going, he knew it would change nothing.

Man found Henry Fielding with his wide shoulders sloped against the wall.

'My father, Mr Man, used to destroy such horses as showed more promise than your friend does today.'

The watchman nodded glumly. 'I had little enough hope before, but this—!'

They both looked over the head of the first witness and towards the seated justice.

' 'Tis said,' Fielding muttered, 'that whenever one asks him how it goes, he replies, "My dear Sir, you see I keep hanging on, hanging on" – and this with the soberest face in Christendom!'

'Well, you have only to look at him now – all the black resentment of one who has just met his wife's new favourite. I'm afraid he does not much love those who love our Savage.'

The train of witnesses continued: erect gentlemen in fine clothes followed by even finer ladies. Justice Page listened to each of them without a word of interruption; but all the time his posture was that of a surly courtier, and his eyes those of a fault-finding tailor. Hunched over his papers in his robes and wig, he had the look of a sore boil just on the verge of bursting.

'What's to be done?' the thief-catcher finally asked.

Man thought a minute. 'Something, perhaps, that concerns your own by-work. Do you see that man over hard by the door there?'

Fielding used his height. 'He with the long pen, is it?'

'The same. Mr Thomas Cooke. The man to his right is his brother-in-law, Mr Beckingham. The first gentleman wrote well of Savage in his *Battle of the Poets* two years past, and since the Coroner's inquest he has been engaged with some others in the making of a short life of Savage. It's hoped that it will help him to gain a pardon – if one should be needed. I thought you might lend them your genius, with what information I can give you.'

'Whatever I can do, of course.' He sounded interested.

The final witness – an impressive amalgam of lace and powder – was gladly dismissed. Then, dividing all his authority between his expression and his voice, the judge reviewed the evidence of the witnesses and the accused. As he neared the end, his voice could have been expected to tremble with an offended heat; but it only lowered itself to an insinuating, oily purr. The peroration especially had such a melodic lilt to it that, listening from his new station at the wall, Man wondered how long it would be before some wit set it to music.

'And now my dear gentlemen of the jury:
You are to consider that Mr Savage is a very great man,
A much greater man than you or I,
                          gentlemen of the jury;

That he wears very fine clothes,
Much finer clothes than you or I,

> gentlemen of the jury;

That he has abundance of money in his pocket,
Much more money than you or I,

> gentlemen of the jury;

But then, my dear gentlemen of the jury,
Is it not a very hard case,

> gentlemen of the jury,

That Mr Savage should therefore *kill* you or me,

> my dear gentlemen of the jury?'

Page concluded by drooping and shaking his head, as if he were inexpressibly weary of this our life, and the sham was sold to the wide-eyed gentlemen of the jury.

But even now Savage was not beaten.

'Am I to stand here, Sir, and hear my case be cheated and perverted until even I can scarcely recognize it?'

Page pretended to search the hall. 'Is there anyone here to tell this fellow he may stand wherever he damned well will, so long as he does it in silence?'

'Even a man as luckless as myself,' Savage fumed, '– as provoked and pushed towards his own undoing – has a claim to equal justice before the law and not to be painted out a monstrous fop!'

'I wonder,' the judge continued, still ignoring him, 'that any man – even a gentleman! – should not understand the sense of the word "silence". Now isn't that strange, though?'

Savage turned to face the jury. 'I repeat, Sirs: If I fled from the scene of the accident, it was only to escape—'

But Justice Page had had enough. Looking off towards the high ceiling, he executed a surprisingly delicate, sweeping motion with his hand, and a burly officer stepped forward to carry Richard Savage bodily from the hall. The prisoner's voice ran on, but grew smaller until it ceased.

That was enough for Man and Fielding, too. Neither expected any great surprises in the verdict, and they wanted to be near the door at the end to anticipate the rush. The trial had dragged on for almost eight hours, and both men hungered for the bracing air of the active streets. The watchman felt suddenly feverish and dry and empty.

They could hear the drier voice of Justice Page behind them, instructing the gentlemen of the jury. Admirable characters counted not a farthing against hard, clear evidence. When two men attack each other, the death of either is determined to be only an act of manslaughter; but when one attacks first – and succeeds in killing the other – the action, however sudden, is supposed by the law to be malicious.

The jury had decided upon their verdict even before Man and Fielding could reach the door.

Justice Page repeated the verdict with wet-lipped relish: a pronouncement of wilful murder against Richard Savage and James Gregory, the lesser charge of manslaughter against William Merchant, because 'he minded not to bring a sword'.

George Man, shouldering his way through the crowd at the exit, ignored the judge's shout for silence, but Page's next words stopped him cold.

'But one thing more, then. Is the Ordinary of Newgate Prison among us here today?'

Man motioned resignedly to Henry Fielding to wait. He knew what was coming, and he didn't like it.

The sad-faced chaplain who had pestered Savage with his prayers excused himself before the bench.

'Did Mr Merchant here hack out the neck-verse for you, Sir?'

Man tasted bitterness. He wondered if this out-of-date practice would ever be laid to rest – this easing of the punishment for certain first offences claimed, as by the churchmen of old, by anyone who could read out a Latin verse from the Bible.

The chaplain hesitated. 'He did, my Lord, near as I could—'

'Right!' The judge was in a sudden hurry. 'Then this court directs that, by Mr Merchant's craving the benefit of his clergy, the letter "T" be today branded into the base of his right thumb. Sentencing of the other two shall be upon the Monday next.'

The watchman and the thief-catcher left first, craving conversation and ale. They knew that the last hope left to Savage and

Gregory was somehow to obtain a free pardon from the Crown. It would be anything but easy: the case against them was too clear, and the trial had been too conclusive. The problem would have to be attacked from more than one direction at once. And as always, there was so little time.

As the two friends turned into Cow Lane, Henry Fielding was promising to begin immediately with the plan that Man had suggested to him during the trial. The watchman said that he himself would try a more direct and bolder method. He expected he would need some help; but he knew, he added, just the right man for it.

'Who's that?'

'Why, Mr William Merchant, of course!'

Chapter 19

It was Man's habit, no matter what his health or business, to visit a barber's every second Wednesday for what his friend Ned Ward would call 'two pennyworth of razoridge'. He liked to sit back with his face bearded with hot suds and let the barber scrape away at him. It could be one of the most relaxing experiences he knew.

But he did not really go there for the relaxation – hardly even for the shave. He went because, in all of London and Westminster, the barber's vied with the chandler's as the best place to gather news. Unlike most men, the watchman rarely patronized the same shop twice in the year. He preferred instead to stop at different shops in different neighbourhoods, usually in whichever area of the city he happened to be working in at the time. Once there, he would talk just enough to appear friendly, but mostly he would listen. (It was anyway ridiculous trying to speak intelligently with your nose pinched between the barber's soapy fingertips.) He never came away without having learned something. The barber near Tower Hill might be vastly different from his brother at Hanover Square, but it was universally acknowledged that all of them were omniscient.

Today Man was seated in one half of a pair of painfully straight-backed chairs in a shop in Little Swallow Street, Piccadilly. The room was tiny and too hot, the soap was cool and flat, and the barber's blade seemed to be made of wood; but a long hallway with an open door at the far end of it gave on to the passing street, and the distant pantomime of cold sunlight gave to the interior a mood of comforting secretiveness. Nothing could happen in here. No one would find you. There was no time.

The barber was a squat bottle of a man who called himself Ben. In appearance, he was an imperfect advertisement of his trade. A wide swath of bare skin ran from forehead to neck, swooping the remaining hairs out and back in a pair of eagle's wings. His beard was the kind that could be shaved three times in a day without any noticeable improvement. A handful of greying teeth was jumbled towards the front of his mouth, splaying his consonants; but they had no effect whatsoever upon the barber's traditional ability to talk without feeling the need to breathe.

Yet now it was the third man who was doing most of the talking. The other chair in the shop was taken by a smart-looking servant in a rich jacket with too much cuff who sat so unnaturally erect that he could have leaned back on a stool without falling. Having already been shaved and powdered, he was now idling away an extra half-hour with a fresh news-sheet spread out upon his knee. He was one of those people who assume that whatever is important enough for them to read must be important enough for all to hear; and he was reading aloud now through the upper reaches of his wide nose, as if he had once been taught that all educated men read this way and he had never let himself forget it.

'Now look ye here next, gentlemen! Here's a warm report on some great doings at the Old Bailey day before last – sentencing of those two mean scoundrels, Savage and Gregory. Either of you there for it?'

A 'Not thish chicken, Sir,' from the barber and a noncommittal 'Mmm' through the suds from Man.

'How's it read, then? Uh – "yet the prisoner Savage presented himself with all the pride and honour due his high birth" – that's him to the life, ain't it? "Mr Gregory stood stiffly silent throughout, praying pardon from his betters with a squinting, meagre, low, hang-dog countenance" – and very like yellowing his breeches as well, if he's anything the same as his heartless friend, Merchant. What next? Ah – "Mr Savage was favoured by the judge with a last opportunity to make a plea for pardon or for clemency" – damned more than the blackguard deserved, too, to my mind.' The man in the chair turned the sheet over and exclaimed: 'Why, my God be damned by all! They've writ the whole of it out for us! You'll want to hear this now, gentlemen!'

'If'snot too mush treble t'ye, Sir,' the barber lisped. 'I'fefer bim one hot fer noose, you—'

'We know that, Ben, we know. Hotter anyway than Savage is for his noose, I'd wager! But haven't you a cup of something in here? I'm all over dust.'

The man was supplied with a dram of watery gin, then he settled himself by cracking his neck back with an audible jerk. The watchman wearily closed his eyes to listen. *I can remember it*, he said to himself, *almost word for word*.

'Now we've come to it. "It is now, my Lord" – this is my Ladyship's famous bastard speaking now – "It is now, my Lord, too late to offer anything by way of defence or vindication" – had his chance for that last Thursday – "nor can we expect aught from your Lordships in this court but the sentence which the law requires you, as judges, to pronounce against men of our calamitous condition." Well, what would the fellow want, then?'

'But whashat condishen there, Sir?'

'Bad, Ben. Very bad.'

Bad for some, yes. Not so bad for another. What is a sore thumb compared with a slow strangling at the end of a rope? A wise trade, that. Wise Merchant. Flies into the room at Robinson's, begins a forged brawl, and Look ye! I fear I've left my sword at home! Convenient. Safe. Most of the other street-porters say that's the size of the man, more mouth than heart. Happy chance for him that Savage and Gregory were there to stand for him. If not . . . But how did Savage come there, then? By accident? The three men could not have met at all, if Dick had stopped at Richmond. The letter. Not from the landlord. But Merchant can read and write. We all know that now, don't we?

The straight-backed man said: 'I'll go on then, gentlemen. Ah – "But we are also persuaded, that as mere men, and out of this seat of rigorous justice, you are susceptive of the tender passions, and too humane not to commiserate the unhappy situation of those whom the law sometimes, perhaps, exacts from you to pronounce upon." That's smoothly argued, I'll grant it. But he's tried the same fawning with my Ladyship, and with as little effect. Now – "No doubt you distinguish between offences which arise out of premeditation and a disposition habituated to vice or immorality" – spoken by one who knows, friends, he having once attempted the murder and rape of his own dear mother. But the porter, I can promise you, is even now carrying news of that earlier outrage to the Queen's own ear. So – "vice or immorality, and transgressions which are the unhappy and unforeseen effects of a casual absence of reason and sudden impulse of passion" – Hah! This is wit. Whose fault is it but his own that he is so beetle-blind that he cannot see what is being done to him – and by whom?'

The man happily lowered his gurgling nose into his cup.

But why choose Savage, and none other, to fight his fight for him? Some resentment? Merchant not the man to forget or forgive. Perhaps planning to use the old vellum to forge the will himself. Stand in the middle and keep both Savage and Bellamy in the dark. Doubled double-dealing. But then Dick steps round him to get to the housebreaker himself. Merchant left empty-handed. Yes, that would be enough. But how could it be made to pay him?

'Ah! Now it comes out!' He belched with satisfaction. ' "We therefore hope you will contribute all you can to an extension of that mercy which the gentlemen of the jury have been pleased to show Mr Merchant, who (allowing facts as sworn against us by the evidence) has led us into this our calamity." And too damned well paid for it, as I was not behind in saying to my Ladyship herself the other night when he sends his whore round to collect for him!'

Man could feel the hot air cold against his shaved skin. The slack-lipped barber busied himself with towels and lotion.

Of course. Vengeance alone not enough for Merchant. But there is someone who might pay well to see Savage in a trouble he could never get out of alive. Someone who might have to make up the six thousand denied him, who is weary of his face at the window, who has had enough of being reminded of past errors. His own loving mother, Anne Brett. She would pay anyone anything.

'Now here's the end on it, men. "I hope this will not be construed as if we meant to reflect upon that gentleman, or remove anything from us upon him, or that we repine the more at our fate because he has no participation of it: No, my Lord! For my part I declare nothing could more soften my grief than to be without any companion in so great a misfortune." And that's the whole of it, gentlemen,' the man in the rich coat concluded, folding up his news-sheet and draining his cup. 'About as nice a piece of rehearsed puppetry as this town's seen this year!'

A puppet-play with Savage cast as the first puppet, Man thought. *Murder by proxy. But why choose James Sinclair as the victim? That benefits no one, William Merchant least of all. Unless . . . Unless the wires are longer than any of us thought, and what the porter is holding are nothing like the ends . . .*

The man in the rich coat took his leave in a flurry of tails and powder, and Man and the barber were left alone in the shop. The small square of street at the end of the hallway was beginning to fade with angling snow.

The watchman thoughtfully shrugged on his coat and paid his bill. As he started to leave, an oily finger tugged at his arm.

'D' you know thet one, though?' the barber lisped, winking as provocatively as a healthy whore. 'He's a fine one, ain't he? Mrs Breth's own stew'rd, he is!'

'That is well for him,' Man answered innocently.

'Comes in here ev'y udder day, he does.' Ben's once-white shirt strained across the puffed chest.

The watchman nodded grimly. 'I know that, Ben. I know.'

Chapter 20

By the time Man got there, the whole square was screaming. Most of the women were screaming in stark panic, probably because for the first time in their lives their panic was real. The men ran about screaming orders at no one, grunting with excess effort, working too fast for fear of not working fast enough. And the children, carried off by the bright wonder of it all, were vying with one another in screaming themselves hoarse: 'The fire! The fire! Look at the fire!'

The fact that it was an early Sunday evening assured an ever-growing crowd. Apprentices and servants, whole families and parties of friends, were free to leave their drinking and talking and eddy about the square, appearing to be concerned or offering theoretical advice. Some of the men even ran forward to join in passing the leather buckets from the fountain to the house, but most of them spent too much of their time grinning back at the ladies they had left at a safe distance. There were far too many heroes and not enough help. And all the while the handsome house at No. 2, Soho Square, kept on consuming itself with lengthening flames.

The watchman would not have come to the square at all, had he not grown weary in the last four days of searching in vain for the missing William Merchant. Man had looked everywhere – in every choking night-cellar, every sweating tavern and bagnio, every meeting-place of thieves and whores in the darkest sections of London and Westminster. He had visited the girl Kitty in her single, windowless room and found her lying speechless with fever and fantasies, obviously dying, attended by a local surgeon who had been busy remorselessly opening every vein he could coax to the surface. She could not help him; no one seemed able to help him. William Merchant had evidently been absorbed into the close, ungiving stones of the city's streets.

It was not that Man had any hopes of finding the porter anywhere near the house of Abraham Sinclair. As far as he could see, there was no possible point of contact between the old importer and the young urban vagabond. It was only that, on his way to look in on Sarah at her father's house, the watchman had been taken with an unaccountable urge to see if he could come and talk with the Sinclair family's last remaining son, Walter. Man could not forget what Ned Ward had said to him about the hidden wisdom of apparent madness.

The house was flaring more methodically now in the glazed air that smelled of promised snow, as if the falling sun had abandoned an ounce of its fire there that could not help but burn. The flames seemed hottest and thickest at the window that Man knew belonged to the father's workroom, and it was to there that the line of men in the square pointed most of their efforts. Yet the elastic heat continued to expand, nudging the people back and turning their faces away as if from an insult.

The watchman had just started going from man to man, shouting if anyone was left inside, when the front door swung fully open and the strange exodus began. The square was flickering with light and noise and crisscrossing forms beneath a lowering, colourless sky. Everyone was frightened; no one was sure of what to do. Man saw one gentleman shivering and weeping. Yet the inhabitants of the Sinclair household now came walking out through the vacuum erected by the fire at the door as calmly and carelessly as if they had been only strolling out for a breath of evening air.

They marched out singly or in pairs. The servants came first in a self-embracing mass – the women with their hair frazzled on end, the men coughing their tongues out. Maids and cooks were met by neighbourly women with cloaks; the others found cups of hot rum or gin thrust into their hands. They were all shepherded towards the iron fence at the centre of the square, where they lay or sat or simply stood mournfully shaking their heads.

Man moved closer to the house, feeling the heat smearing his cheek. The relayed buckets had finally begun to eat away at the roots of the fire, isolating the blaze within the confines of Abraham Sinclair's workroom. The rest of the house was bothered with moiling smoke or vagrant whips of sparks, but the watchman guessed it could be saved.

The wordless shouting around Man flared into a relieved hum as a darker shadow in the smoke-framed doorway congealed into a moving body. It was a small woman – not old, but warped – with a rodent's habit of walking forward timidly in the shape of a wedge. The watchman had never seen her before, but he supposed her to be the importer's current wife, the faceless Anne. She was hurriedly lassoed by a ring of irresistible hands and trundled off into oblivion.

Two more women followed with such eerie regularity that Man wondered if they had been waiting patiently in line in the front hallway. The first was dressed entirely in black – this would be Philippa, still mourning her first lost brother. Then came a taller woman, straight as a stick, with a look of eternal unforgiveness in her mechanical walk. Hester, the spinster. Both these women came out of the fire in perfect control of themselves, moving in the sedateness of a trance. Only from where Man was standing, no more than half a dozen strides from the sooty front door, he could notice the second woman glancing anxiously behind her, fearful for something she had been forced to leave in the blackening house.

Everyone out in the square waited. The fire was tamed, domesticated, into transient smoke. The house stood blank and still and dripping. Something unspoken among the men outside prevented anyone from trying to enter, although two or three circled warily closer to the door, bending over to peer underneath the issuing smoke.

The watchman suddenly ran over to where Abraham Sinclair's head steward was standing, the fellow with the manners of an Irishman.

'Is your master still within?'

The man was trying to control the quivering of his bluish lips.

'He'll be out, Sir, whenever he's a mind to.'

'And the children, Walter and Sophia? What of them?'

'Here's another!' someone yelled to the square.

Man turned and saw.

With the light of the fire smothered and the ink of the night spilling over the tops of the houses into the square, the open doorway was a churning sump of darkness. A charcoal fog swept out of it in fine, combed hairs. A muted roaring still could be heard at its core. A deep pocket appeared at the centre of the smoke – an infernal cavity that had no bottom – and at the heart of this Man could see an inhuman figure of incorporeal shadow taking shape and coming forth with everlasting slowness.

Abraham Sinclair walked out of his smoking house with crabbed determination, despising the ruin and danger around him. He was charred and singed, his unbuttoned shirt showed a blackly powdered wren's chest, for once his face looked darker than his eyes. In front of him, cradled in the hooks of his arms as if they were precious children, he was carrying a stack of smouldering ledgers.

Man took a single step towards him, then stopped. Abraham Sinclair needed help from no one.

The old importer paused for a moment on the threshold, glaring out malignantly at the awed crowd. He seemed to be angrily searching for someone – he sifted through the faces gathered before him like so much chaff – yet those who had already escaped from the house did not interest him. He looked up at the darkness overhanging Soho Square and hated it. Then the liquid flames at his sides took a harsher lick at him, but he shouldered them aside and strode out. They split and fell back before the old man's unflagging, supernatural defiance. They could find no hold on him.

But Abraham Sinclair must have been more deeply shaken than he looked. When the watchman ran over to where the leaders of the crowd had settled him, he found the importer grey with shock and clawing the ledgers closer to his chest with the reasonless frenzy of the panicked. Man almost felt sorry for him, seeing him shivering there with age and disbelief. Almost.

The head steward came running, screaming frantically.

'Mr Abraham, Sir! Mr Sinclair.'

The importer must have heard him – the steward kept shouting it into his ear – but Abraham Sinclair was slow to respond, almost as if he didn't know who or where he was. He stared at the ruining house, remembering. Then he came back to himself.

'And Mr Walter and Miss Sophia?'

'Gone, Sir. They must have left just before—'

'Find them! Bring them back to me!'

Man watched as Abraham Sinclair, with most of the ledgers slumped over on to his stronger left arm, tried testily to button his shirt against the cold. He could not do it without the steward's help, and a recollection of the old workman in the warehouse in Beer Lane suddenly picked at the watchman's memory.

Man was leaving by way of Sutton Street, when he saw somebody running towards an opposite corner of the square. It looked very much like the street-porter, William Merchant.

He ignored him. In the last few days Man had pursued scores of William Merchants down scores of twisting streets, and all for nothing. Right now, the only thing he wanted was a long sleep.

Chapter 21

It was only a minute's walk from Little Turnstile to the Bull and Gate Inn, but Henry Fielding ran it anyway. He had come back to his rooms late today and found the message hours old. A hot excitement made him hurry, but he felt too ashamed to admit it to himself. And he wondered as he ran if he would ever have the courage to tell it to the watchman, George Man.

During the past week, Fielding had done everything Man had asked him to do. The thief-catcher had sat up late with Cooke and Beckingham, with Aaron Hill and Lord Tyrconnel, passing on to them whatever information Man had given him concerning the life and character of Richard Savage. The pamphlet was now ready: *The Life of Mr Richard Savage. Who was Condemn'd with Mr James Gregory, the last Sessions at the Old Bailey, for the Murder of Mr James Sinclair, at Robinson's Coffee-House at Charing Cross.* Several thousands were expected to be dispersed over the nation, and Lord Tyrconnel was now preparing – in direct contradiction to the interests of his aunt – to present Savage's case formally before their Majesties through the influence of his intermediary, Mrs Clayton, mistress of the robes to Queen Caroline. Hopes ran high at Lord Tyrconnel's grand house in Arlington Street, but Fielding himself believed that it would take something more than published praise to save Savage now.

The thief-catcher had also tried, with no success at all, to help Man locate the elusive William Merchant. And, since the burning of the house in Soho Square, he had asked every contact he could find if they knew anything about the present whereabouts of Walter or Sophia Sinclair. He had had no luck there either, no more than the watchman. It was Man's opinion that the two young people were not even trying to hide from them, but from their own father; and that if any man in London could find them, it would be Abraham Sinclair.

And now Henry Fielding was hurrying excitedly towards the Bull and Gate in response to the message in his pocket that was signed by one 'Mr Western'. He knew no man of that name, but he suspected that the name was not important.

The yard of the Bull and Gate ran the length of the building beneath the two floors of balconies from which long poles protruded, hung with flapping, freezing wash. Tonight the yard was alive with coaches and horses and pestering men, the rushing and the jets of frosty breath both foretelling the coming Christmas season. Coaches decorated with the mud of hundreds of miles on their sides sagged with the weight of seasick passengers and sparkling gifts. Everybody was sure they would come late, everybody was sure they had brought just one trunk more. The rattled employees of the inn puffed and screeched and ran into one another, while the landlord swore and stamped and his wife inquired of anyone who would listen why she had ever been born.

Fielding finally managed to collar a winded boy who directed him to a room at one end of the second balcony. The thief-catcher had not even reached the stairs, before a dreadful hammering filled his chest and ears. At the top, he paused to slow his breathing and to look out on to the animated, crystalline scene below him. He thought he might remember this instant for a long time.

He was not really very greatly surprised to discover that 'Mr Western' was Sophia Sinclair. The two had seen much of each other lately, and Fielding had expected her to call for him eventually to help lead her out of her trouble. He had no idea what he could do for her, but he knew that he had to see her again. She was just that exact combination of forced weakness and maddening strength, innocence and wickedness, that Henry Fielding found always so intoxicating.

She was sitting in a chair in the one part of the tiny room which the light of the single candle could not reach. The only other chair had been pulled up dangerously close to hers. Fielding noticed the bed.

As he made an imperceptible bow and lowered his long body

into the chair, he saw that she was leaning forward in a tightening strain of fear and will – her face sallow, her neck and shoulders arching unnaturally, her hands toying incessantly with some small object. He could hear the buried scraping of her breath as if from an adjoining room. There was an eating cold draughting outward from the dead fire, but the clear white handkerchief that covered her upper breast lay slightly disordered – whether by design or accident – and Fielding found himself staring at an oblong of perfect skin, warm as cream.

Sophia Sinclair said only, 'You have come.'

'As you see. You are much missed in the town.'

'By my – father, you mean?'

'And by some others,' Fielding answered uncomfortably. 'Where is he now, do you know?'

'I have heard he is staying at Mr Dodington's while the house is repairing.' A scowl suddenly marred her face. 'But it is nothing to me where he lies or whom he chooses to abuse next.'

'He is your father, Sophy. You shouldn't—'

Her new expression stopped him. He could not understand it. It was as if he had used some word that had long since passed out of use.

Still she examined the object with her hands, but invisibly, in the wash of shadows collected in her lap.

'Was it you set fire to your house?' Fielding asked her gently.

'No.'

'Your brother, then? Walter? But why?'

He could tell the moment her breathing stopped. Then, a long shudder of cold and disgust, and her voice became a man's voice.

'To save himself!'

He expected her to say something more – something hot and wild – but she only sat still as before. Fielding was close beside her, but he thought that even the miniature noises from the courtyard seemed closer and more welcoming.

He settled back against the chair, but it was only to ease the lower half of his body an inch nearer to the wings of her dark skirts.

'Can I help you, Sophy?'

She said at once: 'I mean to go to the Continent. To Leyden. I have a friend, a lady—'

'But what'll you do there?'

'Who can say? Perhaps nothing but wait . . .'

'But your father's trade—' Fielding began.

'– shall never be mine, Sir!'

'Yet after his death . . .'

She whispered to herself: 'He will live to bury us all.'

The thief-catcher could not have said when it happened, but at some time during the last few minutes her right hand had left off its playing to come and settle subtly upon his knee. It did not move, yet it pulled at him somehow.

'Do you really hate your father so?'

'I should not hate my – *father*!' She sounded hurt.

The hand at his knee kept drawing him closer.

'You'll be needing money, Sophy,' Fielding finally offered, 'and I have so little.'

Nothing changed, neither of them moved, only the candle's flame swayed a little as it dwindled – yet the easy weight of her body was suddenly warming his thighs, her thin arms were entrapping his neck, the flesh of her breast was a burning and scented promise against his lips. He could not control his hands.

She told him everything: that her father, who never went out anywhere, was expected to attend the Christmas masquerade at the Opera House with over a thousand pounds in notes in his coat, meant as a delayed payment to Mr Heidegger. Her father hated her, he would give her nothing, leave her nothing; and with her brother James gone, she had no one left to protect her, to be with her and succour her . . .

Young Henry Fielding carried her in his arms across the room, feeling her moving mouth wetting his throat. And later he could not remember how many times he had heard himself saying 'Yes'.

Chapter 22

The tavern in Vine Yard off St Olave's Street, Southwark, had a name held up by an illustrated signboard held up by a century-old ale-pole. The pole and sign hung unaccountably straight and true from a leaning, sagging house that had threatened for decades a massacring tumble into the street, but no one bothered much looking up at the tavern's name on his way in. The tavern was ancient and notorious, both within its neighbourhood and without, and even strangers to Southwark rarely missed it passing by. The roadway itself diverted their steps towards the door – a shallow groove worn by ages of entering boots and departing hands and knees. And there was always the hidden slide of loosened stones held in reserve to trip the disinclined traveller down and through the unclosed door.

But tonight none of these unplanned devices was needed. The signboard was festooned with a single eyebrow of sodden snow that obliterated all the decoration except for a corner of the smock-shaped surcoat and the left half of the letter 'T'. The curving gouge was filled to overflowing, the accidental scree was curdled with scuffled packing; yet the tavern's two windows, mediæval and dingy, vibrated with bilious candlelight and agitated, unsure shadows. The straining walls of the house seemed to be cracking from internal heat and noise; the combined energy of heated men sheltering together made the whole building drone. There was no lack of business tonight. No man in his right wits and mind would want to be out walking in this.

Because tonight the streets of Southwark were a labyrinthine gauntlet of flying and stinging snow, snow that beat at a man and stole the breath from his chest, glued his eyelashes together and stopped his ears, spinning snow that danced him round and round

175

until he didn't know which way was his, clinging snow that pummelled him and punished him until he would want to escape into anywhere – cower into even the lowest hole – just to find himself a place to hide.

Inside was warmth and dryness and the fellowship of men enjoying hard-won comfort. There was among the company that unreal privacy common to the snowbound, the enclosed feeling that the great world had been reduced to a few tables and chairs, a rack of steaming coats, a solitary fire. No man could remember very well where he had been meaning to go – or why – and just now some talk had been heard of blankets being passed round with the next order of drinks.

The two men sitting together farthest from the fire did not need any more gin to warm them. The one in his shirt was hot and red enough already with baking anger; the other sat back in a greatcoat that was buttoned to his throat and padded on all sides with shapeless, insulating bulges.

The street-porter, William Merchant, shook his shirt loose from his neck with the hand that wore the bandage round the thumb.

'Why else do you think, Ned, I've been looking for you these many days?'

Edward Bellamy, the housebreaker from Seven Dials, threw out an arm with a metallic rattle in the sleeve and squinted cutely at the other man.

'Well, now. I'd had some hope it were for love of me, Bill.'

Merchant tasted his mouth sourly and eyed the filthy beggar sleeping across the adjoining table. The tip of the soiled handkerchief that covered the left cheek waved at the snoring. The street-porter was a man who knew something about toothache.

He needlessly massaged his own jaw and said, 'Not that, Mr Bellamy. Not yet. I'm not loving any man that won't stand constant next his friends when he's needed.' The porter moved his hand to his neck to wipe it dry. 'No, I was only wondering how the trade was running for you these times. Sell many new-writ papers lately?'

'Myself? Oh no! Now I haven't touched even one page for – what? – weeks and weeks!' Bellamy shifted forward in his chair to the internal accompaniment of crackling bread. 'You know, Bill, no man's wont to sweat for his reading when he wakes each night from his dreams with that terrible tightness round his throat and his feet still dancing through the dark air. Would you, then?'

The beggar at the next table groaned, bubbled, slept on.

'I thought as much.' Merchant nodded. 'But there's something here, Ned, that you know as well as me: no goods, no script, no ready. You must be wearing a bloody short purse this season.'

'Oh, no fear there, my friend. It'll grow!' The housebreaker smugly patted a pocket that jingled with the muted sound of coins – or loose spoons. 'All it wants's a little time, that's all.'

'But there's none of that for sale at this table tonight, Ned. Not for you, not for me.'

'How's that?'

The housebreaker's unclean face was still cheerful and mocking, although a slow worry had begun gathering at its edges. He had noticed that now the street-porter was keeping both hands under the table.

Throughout the tavern's single room ran a tired but restful mellowness that showed itself as a creamy, uncertain yellow light. In the depths of it, the men sat mumbling their cups and their pipes, nodding ponderously like dozing elephants, and occasionally rousing themselves into a complete sentence or two – rarely more. With the tireless wind scouring the building outside and describing on the windows patterns of needle-sharp snow, there could be no good reason for going out, no good reason for worrying about the rest of the night, no good reason for doing anything. Sitting and drinking and smoking were enough. There was no hurry.

It was the dullness of the atmosphere that affected the housebreaker, made him slow to react, slow to fear. He looked at William Merchant, dripping with heat and building rage, and saw nothing more than a dissatisfied, slightly ruffled street-porter.

Bellamy smiled lazily across his cup. 'But I'm something surprised myself, Bill, to find yourself staying so long in the town. I should have thought after . . .' The housebreaker tipped his head to one side and sighed dramatically. 'Well, you've no worry, eh?

177

If the dad's got another small work for you – hey! You have yourself another thumb for another branding, don't you?'

The beggar next door chortled in his hungry dreams.

'Now, how is it you know so much, I asks myself?' Merchant muttered after having briskly drained his cup. He stared vacantly with the parched desperation of a week's deep drinking. 'No, Sir, you really ought not to know so much of another man's business. Especially as that man's business is the kind that never looks to come to an end.' The porter sat back a bit – but not relaxing – and brought his left hand to the top of the table. It moved there nervously to and fro, but gradually came to settle into a hard gripping of the table's corner. 'But it's a cold town, Ned, d'you know that? Damned cold. A man does what he's told to do – does it in his own way, but well – and what does he get from it? From the great Lady he gets nothing but a great Lady's curses. And from the old whore's bastard – the mad bugger that don't even own his own name – he gets nothing but more promises. "One work more," he hears. "Just one work more, and the money and the home are yours." How many times have I heard that before?' Merchant complained angrily. 'And this next one's got to be on the seas! Do you know how deep the floor of the Channel lies, Ned? Me, that can't swim a straight yard for my life!'

The housebreaker looked more self-satisfied than ever. He grinned mockingly at Merchant and pulled a ball of wilted handkerchiefs from a pocket, unwound one, and waved it in his face.

'You'll be needing this, Bill, if you're wanting to put your finger in your eye this way.'

Merchant froze. 'So now even you smoke me for a laugh. Even now. You that promised to stand where I stood that night.'

And now in the shrinking body of William Merchant something changed, something that had been wound up too tightly too long, something that had to be let loose . . .

And suddenly he had shot to his feet, hoisting the table up and back into the housebreaker's lap, crashing him to the floor, and the porter stood staring at the short knife in his right hand, wondering dully what he was supposed to do with it now.

A moment later and he was out of the door, but his feet had

only barely grazed the floor. It was the beggar with the toothache who had hustled him out into the pricking storm, numbing the blade from his fingers with a brutal twist and choking the collar of his shirt from behind. Merchant felt himself being carried like a doll into an unnamed alley and straightened against a merciless wall, felt a grip at his throat that was colder than the snow, before he fearfully guessed who the beggar was.

'I leave you breath enough,' George Man said, 'to talk.'

And by the time the slapping snow filled the porter's running eyes, he had told the watchman everything he knew.

Chapter 23

At the King's Theatre in Haymarket, this present Monday, being the 25th December, will be a ball. A sufficient guard is appointed to prevent disorders and indecencies and to oblige all persons guilty of 'em immediately to quit the place. Strict orders are given not to deliver any bottles or glasses from the sideboard and to shut them up early. Coaches are desired to come to the Haymarket and the chairs up Market Lane from the Pall Mall. Costumes from Mrs White at the sign of the Harlequin and Scaramouche in Haymarket or in Little Wild Street. From 9 at night until 7: it will be further noted that any person not able to take himself home at the end shall be carried out of the Theatre *as he is*, and his name will be made known to any who care to hear it.

SOME OF THE PLAYERS

Mr John James Heidegger	appearing as	Himself
Mr Abraham Sinclair	"	the Friar
Miss Hester Sinclair	"	Mother Shipton
Miss Sophia Sinclair	"	the Shepherdess
Mr Walter Sinclair	"	the Bedlamite
Mr Ned Ward	"	Don Quixote
Mr George Psalmanaazaar	"	the Mandarin
Mr Henry Fielding	"	the Magistrate
Mr George Man	"	the Watchman

The idea was simple. Take a room such as the Long Room on the west side of the Haymarket Opera House – a single room measuring approximately seventy-seven by thirty-seven feet; stock it with five or six hundred wax lights, diverse buffets, free Burgundies and Champagnes and sweetmeats, two sorts of music and assorted games of chance; and keep several files of musketeers at hand for the preventing of any embarrassing disturbances. Then cram it with over seven hundred revellers from every imaginable level of society, each armoured with the anonymity of a mask or a disguise and each lubricated with drink and talk and meaningless laughter; mix them all together promiscuously with absolutely no thought of decorum or restraint; and keep them going at it frantically until the excitement of novelty gives way to the numbness of exhaustion. What you will have then is a limited scene of barely controlled, hardly believable, but never-to-be-forgotten madness.

The Long Room was hot, that was the first thing. Then there was the fact that there seemed to be no air in it, other than the portion a man carried in with him inside his own lungs, and that bit was soon enough poked or wrung out of him by a wayward elbow or by the awesome rolling of a hooped skirt. Every cornered hat threatened his eye, the universal noise drummed in his chest, the violated spectrum of colours amazed him. Some gentlemen and ladies brought their pets; and before the night was out a man was sure to find something brown and objectionable smeared upon his shoe or a parrot's black tongue bubbling in his wine or to feel a monkey's rubbery finger fiddling about the whorls of his ear. Theoretically, there should have been enough room for all; but at such functions each man's body seemed naturally to expand until it needed three times the floor space it would normally require. And as for the women, there was simply no containing them.

At some few minutes after ten o'clock, John James Heidegger stood rocking back upon his heels at one end of the engorged Long Room and masterfully ran his fingertips over the whole of the quickening assembly. Of all his related accomplishments, this was still his chief joy. He relished every part of it – the indiscriminating press, the charming disorder, all the glitter of finery and wit. Here he could watch over and direct the coming together of lord and harlot, lady and apprentice, unmatched husbands and wives, in all the safe abandon of disguise and deceit. And if a hand strayed wantonly into a bosom or a pair of breeches – if a face were slapped or hot words or swords exchanged – then so much the better, to his mind. The guards were equal to anything, and a little scuffle would add some spice to these bland English souls. He could teach them what passion was all about – for the proper price.

But most of all Heidegger enjoyed the shining loveliness of it all, because then he himself could stand alone in all his supreme, contrasting ugliness. To be visible, he thought, was everything; the method did not much matter.

Heidegger worked the crowd with his eyes. It was not really so very difficult to identify the man or woman through the mask, or at least to determine the type. Many of the costumes were old friends here, of course; but even the newer ones were transparent enough. Birds of a feather: the most richly spangled masks sought each other out, the longest dominos entwined gorgeously about one another, costumes that could not have cost less than a guinea to rent hailed their cousins by name. The outlandish clung in the main to the bizarre; and, at the other end of the scale, the loud and crude stood mostly apart among the loud and crude. Only a small fraction of the people came to the masquerade to hide: far more came to reveal themselves as they would not dare do elsewhere.

The Swiss Count suddenly stiffened and bristled. There, just now crossing at the waist of the room, he had caught sight of a Watchman, complete with staff and winking lanthorn and a hat bent down to obscure the brow. Heidegger thought he could guess who it was, and the audacity of the man made the manager inflate himself with indignation. No man – as any fool should know – no man had the right to appear at the masquerade as himself – except Himself!

With his curls magnificently in flight and his face glaring hideously before him like a beacon, John James Heidegger set out to sift through the unsettling mass of players.

He did not find the Watchman, but he was almost immediately found by a hooded Friar with a ghostly figure of Mother Shipton in tow.

'Mr Heidegger! Sir! I'll have a word with you.'

'Is it you, then?' the manager asked under the flap of the hood.

'I should have thought to find you in black, Sir, or perhaps as the Ruffin himself, after your latest tanning.'

The Friar led him to an oasis near the groom porter's office, where guineas were being traded in chinking laughter. Mother Shipton was the trailing shadow.

The Friar talked by burying his voice more deeply inside the hood and by worming a long-nailed finger into the manager's belly.

'Have you seen my children here, Sir?'

Heidegger looked at Mother Shipton. 'Why, which ones is it you're wanting?'

'The youngest – Walter and Sophia.'

'Are you expecting them, then? Did the each of them take a ticket?'

'I don't know,' the hooded man faltered uneasily. 'I can't say.'

Mother Shipton ducked her pointed hat as if to intervene, but she was overruled by Heidegger's sweeping arm and bellow.

'Look you, Sir! There's more souls here tonight than in all the city's churches of a Sunday. I can hear more groanings and mur-mured prayers of love in an hour than the good God can listen to in a month! Even if you know their dress, we would have as much chance of finding them as a Papist has of becoming Lord Mayor of London! Can't you see? There's more shepherds alone amongst us than threads upon a tailor's table.'

One of them – a craning Shepherdess, searching the crowd from behind a white mask – was at that same moment leaving the north-west corner of the Long Room and veering carefully towards the centre. She took no notice of the pushing all about her, but only glanced at each of the interwoven costumes long enough to make sure it was not the right one. And when she finally paused to look more minutely at one in the distance – a tall and commanding Magistrate in floating robes, also searching, orbiting slowly from an opposite corner – she at once ignored him and kept sedately moving in a rough parabola that would eventually carry her nearer to the groom porter's office. The Magistrate looked and did the same.

Somewhere between them, hidden behind a screen of fluttering ladies, the Watchman followed both of them without moving.

And in a completely separate section of the room a short figure – costumed in the tatters and tin plate, the dirt and painted hen's blood of the hateful, begging Bedlamite – shuffled mindlessly into aghast gentlemen and over the feet of yelping women as if he were deaf and blind. He walked erratically, but always in the same general direction. One hand held an empty bowl; the other was kept covered in the mess of rags.

The Friar was walking Heidegger towards the front part of the Long Room and saying: 'The unexpected loss of my dear son, James, was a blow to me, Sir – a blow! It was a downward turning of Fortune such as I have never experienced since the dark death of my own brother so many years ago. They were both out of my hands, you know. I was helpless.'

'I can feel that, Sir. And this coming so close upon the death of the other lad in the Park.'

The Friar twitched his hood. 'Eh? Well, yes, of course! But James, you see, was so much more of a – help to me in the trade. He was so quick to take over so much of the running of it from me.'

'Yet you are left with Walter, Sir,' Heidegger remarked, but more out of politeness than conviction.

'Walter!' the Friar began, but he was interrupted by a parade of abbesses and savages – and one snickering Jack Ketch – that straggled between him and the manager. After them came a staggering shepherd who cannoned directly into the Friar and then went off, breaking into song.

They had come now into an area of the room that was one of the most densely congested of all. A table of sweetmeats and a wall of labelled wines had drawn great families of players in a thickening flood. One of them was a tall Magistrate who was careful to avoid the hissing light of the candles. He stopped in mid-swallow as the Friar and Heidegger slipped by, though he did not turn to look. Then he delicately wiped his fingers clean and began to move.

'Walter, you say?' the Friar complained. 'He works as well as he can, I suppose, but his head's not in it. That boy would likely cost me as much or more of the trade than he could find. And he has cost me dearly enough already!'

The manager, greeting the crowd, was only half-listening. 'Of course! The lovely Miss Sophia, then. Many of the girls these times step smartly into their fathers' places, do they not?'

'She is unwell, Sir,' the other answered darkly, 'since her brother's going.' He dropped his voice. 'I fear she may soon need to be sent to visit a soldier's sister in Bedlam for her health.'

For a few paces, a gliding Shepherdess followed a parallel course behind a stand of gentlemen in feathered hats.

'Yet it is of Walter himself that I would speak to you,' the Friar said. 'I mean to send him on a long journey to the Continent to search for and buy me some wines.'

'Now that's news, Sir!' The Swiss Count, already smelling a commission, was suddenly interested. 'To France, no? But that's troubled lands right now.'

'I was thinking more of your own country, Sir, or its closer neighbours. You should know some of the growers there, or another who does.'

'Of course, of course, none better, Sir. Yet even there's hard society for a man as – well, as young, you know, as Mr Walter.'

The Friar casually kicked a dog out of his way: 'He's going notwithstanding.' And the manager understood. 'Now, Sir, as to this other matter. The payment. I have the notes with me now.'

'Not here, my friend,' Heidegger said, briskly taking charge and the other's arm. 'We'll just step up to my offices here.'

A muttered word was enough to leave Mother Shipton wilting at a standstill. The two men curved off towards a corner staircase.

The Friar was not as adept as the Count at working his way through the bramble of disguises. He pushed too hard and never gave way, never stepped aside to miss a collision or used a friendly hand as a cushion against an interfering back. Sometimes he walked too fast, sometimes too slowly, so that he was always either bumping into someone ahead of him or being bumped by someone coming from behind.

Just here, for instance. The Friar had slowed, but not much, and abruptly felt a strong push from a Magistrate at his back that sent him fumbling into a white-masked Shepherdess in front. The girl had to lift her hands to his chest to ward him off. A steadying pressure, and she was gone.

Off to the side, the Watchman was looking on with the knowing smile of a father seeing his first child accomplish its first step.

The Friar did not think to feel beneath his habit until he was almost to the stairs. Then he stopped, patted himself all over, and turned to whisper to John James Heidegger.

'Sharks!' the manager shouted to the room. 'You guards! Over here! There's sharks amongst the crowd!'

In the clatter that followed, no one noticed that the scruffy Bedlamite had bent to pick up something he had dropped – something glinting and metallic – though the tin plate was still tied snugly to his left arm.

Chapter 24

Don Quixote was as mad as a swearing weaver.

'I don't care a bent pin what you say, Sir! Abe Sinclair will see no more of my money. It's my thought that a man ought to show some least liking for his own son, no matter how far outside the marriage-bed he may have got him.'

It was now well past two, and the masquerade in the Long Room had just surmounted its first bout of feverish exhaustion and emerged stronger and gayer than ever. The turmoil of the robbery had been pacified by the entertainment of cold meats and warm drinks at eleven, replaced by the sword-play at twelve and the near-rape at one, and forgotten altogether in the round of spontaneous dancing at two. The guards had returned to leaning up against one another at the wall, and the manager had resumed his cheering circuit of the room, a disfigured face almost black with exhilaration his only mask. And after a few minutes of swearing in Heidegger's office, the Friar had come back down to prowl fuming through the players, a whimpering Mother Shipton at his rear. He was looking for the Shepherdess.

Don Quixote was a stocky man whose worm-eaten tunic of greenish leather and drooping hose might have fitted him better forty years earlier. He wore a crested helmet over an orange handkerchief on his head and carried an ancient, seven-foot halberd as if he were despairing of ever finding a place to set it down. His cheeks kept enlarging themselves alternately, while his chin waggled behind a pasted triangle of inked straw. Periodically, the Knight would drop his gaze and mournfully look about him for an open space of flooring.

He was standing at the deepest end of the room and talking hotly to another man who was dressed in a length of red robe with what was supposed to be a sailing dragon stitched into the back of it. The Mandarin's face seemed as yellow as one of the wax lights, but it was not the effect of birth or paint. He was as sick as any man could be on his feet, and he did not look as if he could stay upright much longer.

'Is it James you are calling a bastard, Sir?' he asked, his hand comforting his brow. 'But I had always thought—'

'James my arse, man!' The Knight waved his lance. 'Do you stand there and tell me that you still don't understand the whole sense of it? Why, how many pages of a book must you read, Sir, 'fore it comes clear to you?' The Don expanded his voice with all the blustering certainty of one who has only recently been told the truth himself. 'It's this street-porter, Bill Merchant, I'm telling you about. He's at my place now with a throat on him that's bruised near as wide as my thigh and two cracked shoulders and a watchman at his side to see that he doesn't run – though he can't. And a doctor has been in six times these last three days to tell him – in words that I myself can't understand a single syllable of – that his days of swallowing meat and bread are over. Though I can't see that it can make much change to him,' he added with a huff, 'who's never looked after any meal he couldn't pour.'

The Mandarin was still trying to get past his first astonishment. 'You tell me that this man – this common murderer – is a natural son to Mr Sinclair himself? But how is such a thing possible?'

'Sir,' the Knight intoned, rolling his eyes, 'if a man at your age still needs to be told – well, the worst of it is that now the old dog won't even help the boy or ease his coming ride inside the cart to Tyburn.'

The Mandarin swayed. 'He's to be hanged yet after the branding and all? But for what?'

'Ah, now, there it is!' Don Quixote unsettled his helmet with his eagerness. 'Let me tell you Sir—'

But just now the Knight was interrupted by a facetious, teasing dame in the guise of a nun who came up to beg his help in rescuing a giggling damsel from a charging clergyman. She led him off by the lance, trailing his breathless protests behind her like a thread through the maze of restless players. The Mandarin was left more or less alone.

He told himself for the twentieth time that he should not have come tonight. Nothing in the gaiety or the lights, the noise or the brilliance, could alleviate any of the nausea that made every inch of his skin feel electric and raw. Something tremendous and final seemed to be happening inside his body, and he felt somehow afraid to let it happen here at this hollow masquerade. No one here could understand his suffering. He needed to be home.

But instead of making directly for the door, the Mandarin set off into the heart of the crowd. The Knight had told him that the Watchman was somewhere in the room tonight, and there was something he had to tell him before it was too late.

He finally spotted the long watchman's staff circling slowly round the edge of the massed players. The Watchman was moving in no particular direction, surveying the masks and the dominos, but with all the taut attention of a stalking hound. He even seemed to catch sight of the Mandarin coming up behind him.

'You appear, Sir, to be going rather badly down before the wind tonight.'

'I am that, Mr Man. It's the season that affects me most, I think. Too much strained jollity.'

The Watchman looked surprised, but sympathetic, and the Mandarin began to follow him in his methodical review of the room.

'I should not have guessed,' the Chinese said cautiously, 'that such entertainments as these were quite to your liking.'

'They are not, but I go where my work takes me, Sir.'

'You are working again, then?'

'I am a watchman,' the other answered with decision, 'even during those times I am not officially called to it. A man cannot change what he is.'

The Mandarin looked away. 'Though some have tried, Sir, some have tried.'

The two men passed through a gauntlet of coy ladies and falsely complimenting gentlemen.

'And has our host, Mr Heidegger, yet seen you in the dress of your trade?'

'I think he has,' the Watchman said and pushed up his hat an inch to smile. 'And I may say I think it has made tonight's masquerade a most specially memorable one for him!'

The Mandarin laughed at just the right volume, but he was obviously thinking of something else.

After another minute of leisurely walking, he asked: 'And are you looking for someone tonight?'

'I am . . . looking.'

'For Mr Abraham Sinclair perhaps?'

'For him perhaps – or at him.' The Watchman turned on the Mandarin. 'But what makes you name that man over any other?'

'I don't know.'

The Watchman seemed ready to let it pass, but the Mandarin was suddenly urged on by a hot spasm of pain so deep within him that he could barely recognize it as his own.

'Well, Sir, I have just this minute been talking with Mr Ward, and he has told me news that I can hardly believe even now.' He stopped to disengage his robe with a dozen bows from the net of a swinging fan. 'Where am I, then? Yes. Well, he tells me that this convicted porter – this Mr William Merchant – is a bastard son of Abraham Sinclair. Is it true?'

Carefully, the Watchman said: 'It would appear that Mr Sinclair has been these past years very busy at peopling this city with his unclaimed sons and daughters. You told me yourself, Sir, that he is a man of unnatural energies. The children are the unwanted fruit.' Through the din of the Long Room could be heard a terrible bitterness in the Watchman's voice. 'There was another of these sons who was brought to the same kind of end that may soon be reserved for Mr Merchant. Another William, as it happens, only this one was found as a hungry boy in the streets by a tradesman named Hawksworth and kindly reared as his own. I have this news only lately from his supposed sister in Bedlam, who has been kept there all these years by regular payments from an unknown hand. She was no more mad, Sir, than you or I – at the beginning!'

Now the Mandarin seemed to feel a new aching that collapsed his body about the hands he carried folded together in front of him. He could scarcely bring himself to speak.

'But what can it all mean, George?'

The Watchman would not answer, but continued his implacable prowling that now brought them both to the happy gaming at the groom porter's office. Yet there was something in his silence, in his stern calmness, that seemed to draw the words out of the Mandarin. He felt as if the two of them were alone.

'Do you recall that advertisement I brought to your rooms in October?'

'Of course.'

He tried to make himself even smaller. 'Well, it was written and published by – by Abraham Sinclair himself.'

The Mandarin thought that the constant noise of the room somehow lessened.

'I suspected as much early on, but I didn't think you would know. When did you learn of this, Sir?'

'I knew – ' he heard himself moan – 'I knew the truth of it from the first. I knew that Abraham Sinclair wanted to frighten James out of his coming marriage – or, better yet, to scare the girl away from him. The father, I think, sees any such union outside the family as something of a personal betrayal of himself. He would be prepared to do almost anything—' The Chinese shook his head wildly. 'But I don't know. I thought he meant it as a private warning to his son, both for the marriage and for the business the boy had taken out of his hands.'

'Then why was I chosen to protect the son?'

'I supposed at first it was only the father's effort to gain more favour with Mr Heidegger, who is so grudgeful against you, by troubling you without cause in something so small. Then, after, I understood that he wanted to involve you in something greater – the death. But now I think there was always more in it.'

'Another private warning?' asked the Watchman.

'Well, you see,' the Mandarin said weakly, 'some days before the killing I was talking to Sinclair's steward – he's a Teaguelander from Dublin and he dearly loves his talk – and he told me that one night at supper Abraham Sinclair was jesting with his son, calling you the boy's own shadow and saying that he had best take care or you might fall upon him yourself. But it was only a joke, can you understand that? Only a part of the gentle bickering and taunting that goes on in all families. I really could not think it anything more.' The Mandarin quailed. 'I was wrong.'

The Watchman had to force himself to look at him.

'You knew all this then – you knew all this even after the murder of James Sinclair – and yet you never came back to tell me? Drury Lane calls you, Sir. You act your parts so well!'

'My parts? But—' the Watchman turned away from him with loathing – 'but I have been practising all my life.'

For some time now, around the walls of the Long Room, had been growing an insistent bustle of ladders and men and a soft thickening of shadows. Over three hundred of the wax candles were being painstakingly snuffed out in preparation for the long-expected exchange of Christmas gifts. Most of the players were hoping to give something to people they could not normally even speak to, and they appreciated the equalizing darkness.

The Friar hated it. He was making still another tour of the room – this time towards the centre, where he was sure he had detected a shepherdess and a magistrate together – and now the draping shadows and the whispering excitement made it all the harder for him to get at them.

He felt tired and angry, for once even tired of his anger, strangely emptied of the blazing energy that had kept him going all these years. He was condemned to walk a neverending hallway that had no exit. In an insight that was decades too late, he knew that he was old.

He was standing undecided in the middle of the throng, disappointed in the disappearance of his prey, when a player dressed in an exotic red robe brushed by and thrust a small parcel hard into his chest. The man was gone in a breath, and the Friar was left holding his own Christmas gift.

More out of weary spite than curiosity – and because it might contain something of value – he opened it and found some cash, a heavy watch, a gleaming woman's ring. There was a note which he had almost to close his eyes to read: 'From Your Loving Sons, James and Walter.' The writing wavered in his old, quavering hand.

The Friar looked about him dumbly, then raised his head and

saw the Watchman advancing solemnly towards him.

He ran.

He was running, and the drumming of blood in his ears was a new sound that dampened all others – the screams, the exclamations, the rasping of a dog – all others, except the quick footsteps that gained on him and grew in number and strength as they drew nearer. He was running with a throbbing lump swelling his throat, through an underbrush of shoulders and hands, dodging past surprised bodies and startled cries, twisting to burst through fragmented conversations. He stumbled and ran on, something fell to the floor and broke, he thought the heaving of his chest would break him, he no longer thought of anything, not even of escape. Only running.

He saw the door growing larger. The crowd fell apart for him. His teeth were cold, bared in a grin or a leer. Every part of him stretched itself forward, thin as beaten tin. He had made it through.

Only then two small things blinked and blinked off to his right – the first round as a plate and dull, the second sharp and sparkling – and then he felt the very centre of his chest being sucked horribly inward, caved clear back to his spine, an unbearable pressure took hold of his lungs and compressed them flat, his heart changed to dust, the floor was beating savagely against his back, he could not run.

From somewhere near or very far away, a woman's voice that he should have been able to recognize was wailing: 'Craven!'

Now he could hear nothing but the inward, rushing river that would drown him. There was an oval of round faces suspended above him, but completely noiseless. Then it parted, and the ballooning face of the Watchman was delicately lowered towards his own. It was a mask with a naked skull hiding behind it, the lips were worked by clever levers, the voice was a physical mass with heat and weight instead of sound. And lying straight and sinking more and more deeply into his own dark cold, he searched for and found the last concentrated fire in himself and translated it atom by shrinking atom into words he could not hear.

'I'm – still – alive!'

But he was not.

Chapter 25

Dry snow floating noiselessly down at night always made George Man think of endings. It was not a bad thought: there was nothing any more wrong or unnatural about an end than there was about a middle or a beginning. Each was entire and perfect in itself; each was where it should be. The end of anything – a man, people together, a time – belonged to the whole; it assured its being what it was. The watchman thought more in terms of completion than conclusion, more of fulfilment than depletion. If a process had any meaning at all – and there was always some – what was the process without all its parts?

A great snowfall in the dark somehow always made Man feel older, but that was all right, too. Each additional year only made him seem more solid, more settled and rooted to the ground. Living and working as he did so much out of doors, he had transplanted into the city the country habit of marking the years by the waxing and ebbing of the separate seasons. And it was the winter, the deepest part of it, that made him feel the most tranquil with its quietness, the most thoughtful with its long dark.

It was about eight o'clock on the eve of the Epiphany when Man turned into Ironmonger Row and slogged contentedly through its grey, rounded drifts. The night was almost warm, a memory of light was the only other moving thing in the street, from somewhere inexplicably far away came the brittle ringing of miniature bells. The watchman felt good about himself tonight, and it was not only because of the soothing effects of the covering muffler of snow. The day had been a successful one, and he thought he could now begin to see the end of Richard Savage's protracted troubles.

The bake-shop of Alice and Walter Kettilby was a secret and

inviting yellow glow behind the rich icing of a wind-piled drift. There was a beacon of light in their shop at almost any hour, and by a mysterious association of the senses it always seemed to emit the toothsome flavour of slowly browning bread. Man trudged happily towards it, growing hungrier at every step and already briskly planning the complicated construction of his night's fire.

He had almost reached the front of the house before he noticed the uncertain light trembling behind the window of his own rooms.

Alice Kettilby must have been watching for him through one of her renewable peepholes, for she ran out wrapped in a shawl and flour to greet him in a valley between two sculpted hillocks.

'You're late to come to home, Mr Man. There's one up the stairs been waiting these long hours.'

'As I see. Who is it, then?'

'A lady, but sure no one that Mrs Man should need to feel herself any jealousy against.' The bake-woman bundled herself, sending out a dusting of flour to mingle with the powdery snow. 'And will your good woman be back again amongst us soon, I hope?'

Man started up the stairs. 'In a day or two, yes. Her mother is gladly mending of her sickness.'

'So you've been there with her all the day today, have you?' the woman persisted, her curiosity warming her against the cold.

Man turned and said in a tone of profound mystery: 'I have all this day, Madam, been in private conversation with Mrs Clayton herself, she who is mistress of the robes to the present Queen. She even,' he intoned awfully, 'poured me out tea with her own hand!'

The watchman was up the steps and through his door before Alice Kettilby remembered to close her mouth and dash back into the bake-shop.

With some disappointment, Man found a modest fire already laid in the main room and the keen chill of the night already dulled. But he did not find his visitor so easily, even though there were so few chairs to choose from and he knew every shadow and odour in the room by heart.

And that was how he finally found her, by her smell – the

distinctive, but not unpleasant, sodden mustiness of the very old and the very worn. She was sitting perfectly still in his own favourite chair, and she seemed so weightless and insubstantial that Man had to come quite close to make sure he was not alone. He almost reached out to touch her.

'Madam?'

He supposed she was asleep, but the old have so little time for sleeping.

'Sir.'

It was the ancient, ageless woman whom the watchman had seen coming into Andrew Millar's bookshop last October. He could not remember her very well, but he did not think she had changed any. She would never change again. Even at the moment of her death, no one would be able to notice any change.

'I am George Man, Madam.'

'And I, Sir,' she said neutrally, 'am Mrs Charlotte Sinclair.'

The watchman was not as surprised as he might have been. He had been feeling all day this abiding sense of termination, and now he was about to find an ending where so many of them could be found – in the beginning.

'Might I bring you something? Tea? A cordial?'

'I want for nothing, Sir, I thank you.'

Man himself felt badly in need of some brandy, but he did not want to disturb the suspended mood of the room by going to get it.

He sat down in his wife's chair and tried to focus on the old woman. As bodiless as she was and in the twilight of the room, she was hardly there at all.

'I should like to ask you, Madam, if you were the mother of the late Abraham Sinclair?'

'I bore him, Sir.' The watchman felt as if he had been somehow corrected.

'For what purpose,' he asked her slowly, 'have you come here to see me today?'

Still sitting upright in her chair, Charlotte Sinclair seemed to concentrate her child's body into a hard mass.

'I want you, Sir, to tell me everything you know about

the deaths of Abraham and James Sinclair.'

Man balked. 'As yet I do not know the whole of it so well, Madam, and now is anyway not the proper time to—'

'Then I shall continue to sit here, Sir, until you think the proper time has come.'

The watchman sat forward with his elbows on his knees to try to see her a little better. She was the most lifeless living being he had ever seen, and after a few minutes he decided to tell her everything. She could wait for ever.

'Your – Abraham Sinclair was killed at the Christmas masquerade by his own son, Walter. The true reasons for this may be lost for ever in that young man's darkened mind, but he does appear to have been horribly frightened of his father – so much that he seems to have taken the father's life in frantic defence of his own. He had tried earlier to burn him in his home, and the failure of that carried him to the more desperate decision to strike directly. I think the boy's dread must have been building in him for long, but some recent event brought him at once to the edge. That event, I should think, was the killing of his brother, James Sinclair, on the twentieth of November last – a murder that was *performed* before my own eyes by a good friend of mine, Mr Richard Savage.'

None of Man's words had as yet made the faintest impression upon the old woman. She sat with her eyes opened or closed, listening or not, her wasted body not even moved by breathing. She might have been made of dead stone.

The watchman pushed reluctantly on. 'I say "performed", because I now know that the death of James Sinclair and every step that led up to it had been all carefully designed and arranged by a young street-porter named William Merchant. He told me so himself, because—' Man hesitated – 'because he had to. He told me how he had tricked Savage into coming into town that night, waited for him and fuddled him with drink, led him with another man to Robinson's Coffee-House at Charing Cross, and then himself created a needless brawl with a total stranger – James Sinclair – who had been deliberately steered there by the porter's girl about town.' Man searched for the remembered scene within the ingrown glare at the roots of the fire. 'He carried no sword himself – that was wise. He shouted, he maddened, he made a quarrel where there should be none. Then he ran behind Savage – I thought to hide – but then he seemed to be trying to hold him back, stop his sword-arm. Yet in the loud madness of that moment, which of us could have distinguished a frantic pulling from a subtle push?'

The fire sank even further into itself, and the watchman found himself talking to an invisible silence.

'You must understand, Madam, that it was clear to me early enough why Merchant should have chosen Savage as his–his pawn. The street-porter is a bullying coward, he felt himself betrayed and robbed by Savage, and a certain Lady had promised to pay him well for involving Savage in a deathful trouble. I could see all this in the porter. Merchant is one who will stay at nothing.' Man paused in thought. 'But I struggled long to understand why he should have picked upon James Sinclair as his prey, a man he could hardly have known before that night. If he had not finally told it me himself—'

Now the old woman interrupted him without warning, her words as weary as the drifting snow outside.

'But the advertisement, Sir. The warning. You could not have thought it came from the porter. Or did you lay it to the dead hand of the almanac-maker, John Partridge?'

Man was embarrassed. 'Of course not, Madam. Though after the killing there were many who thought the concurrence a ghostly wonder, nothing more. I myself felt a different mystery. The advertisement, you will recall, spoke of James Sinclair as the "first son" of Abraham. My first and longest thought was that it was nothing beyond a mistake, an ignorance of the earlier death of Jacob. I could not see it for what it was –' Man lowered his voice to a rasping whisper – 'an old man's forgetting not to say the truth.'

The old woman muttered: 'I knew from the first it was his.'

'Was that the reason for your coming into Mr Millar's bookshop in October? To be certain in your mind?'

'Yes – no. I – meant to leave something for him there. He has never suffered me to come near him . . .'

The watchman thought he could hear a new shading in her words now, the echo of a forlorn pain that had no bottom. Her voice sounded barely human – or all-too human.

Musing aloud, Man continued. 'So William Merchant must have had some private reason for arranging the death of James Sinclair. Too much afraid to do it himself, he at first hired a housebreaker named Edward Bellamy to strike the blow for the sum of twenty-five pounds. To get the money to pay for it and to have some left to carry him into the country, the porter tried to bubble my friend, Mr Savage, by offering to sell him something that he did not have to sell. But soon the housebreaker and Savage struck hands between them, and Merchant was left badly in the lurch. Yet he still had to carry it through. His ingenuity surprises me, the way he was able to invent a plan that would doubtless leave him with no worse than a brand in the thumb. He must have inherited his mean craftiness from his–his father.' Man was uncertain how much the old woman knew, so he decided reluctantly to spell it out. 'You knew, I take it, that your son had promised his natural son, William Merchant, a place in his family for the successful murdering of his lawful son, James Sinclair?'

Man sensed a hopeless, mournful nodding he could not see.

'As I knew he had ordered the death of little Jacob in the Park, as I knew he must someday work the end of poor Walter, as I knew he would heartlessly claim the life of his own mother or of anyone that tried to interfere . . .'

'Sophia's as well?'

'No, Sir, you do not yet understand. He was never so jealous for his trade as most say. It was only for the gain. No, the girls have always been safe enough. Often they have been too – safe.' The old woman's breath gagged in her throat.

Sitting across from her, Man felt the numb and weakening bewilderment of the countryman struggling to understand the calls and dances of an unknown animal.

'But why, Madam? Why should your son wish and plan for the deaths of his own sons, but not of his daughters? I cannot see why any man should ever want to kill any of his children!'

There was an uneasy rustling from the chair, as if a sack of withered leaves were being agitated from within.

The voice, too, was dry and brittle. 'You still do not see it, Sir. You still cannot know how much my son . . . No. But how could you know it? How could anybody?' For the first time, Man heard her faltering in uncertainty. 'None of his daughters – I mean, none of the girls in the family could ever carry the Sinclair name away with them. They could never rob him of what he had worked so hard to get and keep. But the boys – the boys could take a part of the name with them, spread it thin over the land, through the coming years, leave him emptier . . .' The old woman strained to make the inexplicable clear. 'I think it worsened when he grew old. I know: long age does this to so many, leaves them fearful of leaving the family behind and living without them. As if the world itself should fall and die when they do! And Abra—' Charlotte Sinclair stammered weakly – 'my son, Sir, felt it deeper than any other. How can I make you see it? He was one of us – and he was not. He was within the family, and without it, at the one moment. He had so little left him to lose.'

She stopped, run down like an exhausted clock. Not another sound in the room, even the tired fire keeping quiet, the whole house sinking beneath the accumulated burden of snow and anguish.

Suddenly she coughed her chest clear to go on, but Man decided he should save her the agony of having to tell it all.

'Precisely in which year, Madam, did Abraham Sinclair perish in the fire?'

He got little reaction from her. Perhaps a single, hurting sigh, nothing more.

'You know, then. Abraham – the son of my husband, John Sinclair – died late in the summer of sixteen-ninety-nine.'

'In the same house?'

'In King's Square, yes.' The old woman still used the earlier name for Soho Square.

Man clasped his hands together in his lap. He could feel the blood pulsing thickly through the fingers.

'Tell me about his brother,' he said simply.

'My first son was Craven. Two years before Abraham. He –

was not my husband's.' Now the old ashes of her voice began to find a little lost warmth in the remembering. 'John was away so much to sea, you know. There was a young printer's apprentice living in our street: Thomas Howe. He was tall, fine, gay. I was lonely, silly. I loved him. I loved them both. They both fell in the plague. The same week.'

She was so terribly old, with so many years of loving and misery behind her, Man wondered if she would ever find any rest.

The watchman interposed a small detail. 'The two boys used different hands, didn't they? Abraham, his right; Craven, his left.'

Charlotte Sinclair made the lovingly patient sounds only mothers can make. 'Poor little Craven was always so shamed by it.'

A man can change almost anything in himself, the watchman thought, except that.

'And your husband, Madam,' Man asked as gently as he could. 'Did he know the truth?'

The old woman was slow to answer. 'He – never let me know. I think he did, but he was always too good and kind a man to twit me in the teeth with it. Yet from the first he seemed colder towards Craven than Abraham, even though Craven was the first-born son. And his last words left the wine trade to Abraham, too, though I hoped it was only his seeing better business in the boy.' Another sigh – the most tired breathing Man had ever heard. 'Losing all the trade, I think, was what broke Craven, blackened him; but he was always black, vicious, hurtful.'

'When did Craven learn who he was?'

'Who can say, Sir? Who can say? As a young man, perhaps, in some letters from my mother that I let lay too loose around.'

The same as Savage. Nothing new.

'What sort of man was Abraham?' Man asked her.

'Oh, a fair and decent and caring man.' She said it quietly, with a strengthening pride. 'He built up his father's trade and made it his own. And he married a woman, Sir, full as good as himself. They had the girl, Hester. But then the mother died, and his loneliness hurried him to another wife.' The old woman seemed to grow even smaller in the dark. 'I never liked Stella. I – saw too much of myself in her.'

'Whose child was Philippa?'

'More of Craven's dark work, Sir. He stole his brother's wife, because he was not strong enough to steal the trade. Abraham was too good to guess the truth of it.'

'And Jacob and Sophia?' Man had to hear it all.

'No, no! The twins were Abraham's,' she answered desperately. 'I was always certain of it! Both clean babes and true, with none of Craven's deep poison in them. They had to cut them out of her, and dying for them was the only good thing she ever did. But Abraham—Abraham was killed before they were born.' She groaned brokenly. 'My boy could not live to see his only son!'

'And by that time,' Man prompted her delicately, 'Craven had died and come back as Abraham.'

'Who was there to gainsay him, then? It must have been Stella that helped him set the fire, Hester loved him all the more for it, and Philippa was still too much of a prattler to know. And the body – I saw it – no one could . . .'

'There was yourself, Madam.' Man felt a monster for saying what needed to be said.

'He was my bastard,' she murmured, and all the pain in the world filled the room, 'but it was me that made him it. Who can call a man a bastard, without calling the mother a whore?'

Then Man knew the mammoth burden of too many years, the awful immortality of a single mistake that can never be put right.

Man himself sighed now. 'The boy, Walter, must have known.'

'From Hester, yes. They were close. It was that that sickened him, I think.' The fire was all but dead now. 'But it changed Craven worse. He had the family, the trade, everything he had always wanted; but he knew he was not Abraham, and Craven was long dead. And he was so old . . .'

Her last words lengthened on and diminished until they dropped and melted coldly into the unseen floor like snow.

The watchman sensed that they had finally reached the end, but then Charlotte Sinclair roused herself again.

'Can they be helped still, Sir – these men who are meant to hang for James's death?'

'I promise you, Madam, their Majesties are even now hearing

the whole of it. I expect that Mr Savage and Mr Gregory will be granted their free pardons on the morrow.'

She suddenly reached down into the dark lake at her feet and handed across to Man a bulky package, neatly roped and tied.

'I have a work for you, Sir. Here is over one thousand guineas that he has sent me these many years for my silence. I kept my silence for my own reasons and never used a farthing of it. I would have rather starved, Sir – I have starved – than have owed a moment's breath to him.' She stood up then, but she was so small and so faded that it made almost no difference. 'Sophia is still young. They are for her. The only one worth saving from a damned and buried family.'

He walked her silently to the door. He thought of the wet drifts and the blinding night outside, and he told her he would take her to her home.

He could hardly hear her words. 'See only to the money, Sir, and I will bless you. What are the dark and cold to an old woman God has long since forgot?'

Man insisted and turned to get his coat. When he came back, he was alone, and he was not even sure he had heard the door open and close. But the room was colder.

Chapter 26

Came a freshening March with a high sky and shredded clouds and sun, and Man was walking alone through the eastern fringe of St James's Park. For the first time in too many months he was well-fed, well-drunk, and well-satisfied. He was content with the glittering openness of the city today – the highlighted stones and the hollering children – and with the taste of scoured metal that the free wind left in his mouth.

He was marvelling how so many matters had come right, naturally and almost without effort. He had breakfasted this morning at his home with Richard Savage and James Gregory. The two men had been released on bail as early as the twentieth of January, but they had not been able to plead their pardon in court and see the bail discharged until just over a week ago. They were finally at liberty again, and it gave a special tang to Alice Kettilby's glowing bread and raw ale and to the men's carefree talk.

The street-porter seemed much the same as always, but more awakened and relaxed, as if he had just unshouldered an aching load and dunked his head into a trough of shivering water. The watchman noticed a more substantial change in Savage. He was thinner, but less hollow; stronger, but less bantering than before. Elated at his late deliverance, he now swore to devote all his days to his poetry and finally lay aside his futile yearning for a title. Man believed him, though he could not help noting that even now Savage was rushing a poem into print that was 'inscrib'd with all due reverence to Mrs Brett, once Countess of Macclesfield' and provocatively entitled *The Bastard*. The poet himself saw no contradiction here, and Man was too happy for his friend to point it out to him.

Along with his claim to the family, Savage had been forced to give up all hope for any part of his father's estate. The house-breaker, Edward Bellamy, had been taken in Seven Dials by the always-cheerful watchman, Simon Chubb. In the thief's coat had been found, along with a few forks and some filthy oyster shells, a forged codicil to the will of the Earl Rivers that was even clumsier and less convincing than the one that had been dis-covered in William Merchant's rooms. As it happened, Bellamy had never taken anything from Mrs Brett's house but a handful of dirty handkerchiefs and a sheaf of unpaid bills. The housebreaker was sitting now in Newgate, gaily pocketing everything in sight, determined to become the heaviest felon ever to be hanged at Tyburn. There, the weightiest men made the quickest deaths.

Two deaths had already taken place. William Merchant and Walter Sinclair had been scheduled to be carted up Holborn together, but the street-porter had been left to make the journey alone. The last son of the Sinclair family, inept to the end, had fearfully dosed himself with too much laudanum, tried to vomit it up and failed, and finally fallen into a long coma. No one was with him when he died, the unknown ancient woman having arrived at the doors of the prison a minute too late.

Nothing, after all, had turned out quite so well as Man's own work. Now he was being officially called to the parish watch once more, and he had young Henry Fielding to thank for it. Towards the end of January had appeared a sixpenny verse satire, *The Masquerade*, addressed to 'C-t H-d-g-r' and attributed to the pen of Lemuel Gulliver, 'Poet Laureat to the King of Lilliput'. There was nothing so very scandalous about the pamphlet, and John James Heidegger never turned down free advertisement. But Man, suspecting that Craven Sinclair had paid Heidegger to be his eyes that night at Robinson's Coffee-House, had got Fielding's perm-ission to hint at another version of the poem which would surely reach the stalls if the watchman were not reinstated. The ruse had been a weak one, but it had worked – not least because the 'First Minister of Masquerade' had other troubles now that worried his pocket more than his pride. Since the twenty-ninth of January, he had seen his crowds at the Opera House fly to a new kind of opera

– a 'beggar's opera', of all things. Now they could talk of nothing but Captain Macheath and Miss Polly Peachum, and the Swiss Count was looking uglier than ever.

As he started to come out of the Park, Man reflected that the misfortunes of Richard Savage had proved an odd touch of luck for Henry Fielding. Here was Fielding – a rough young man from the country, impetuous, blunt, still unrefined by the city – and he had already managed a minor triumph. His first play, *Love in Several Masques*, had lately been accepted by the Theatre Royal with the famous Anne Oldfield and Robert Wilks in important roles. It was not always easy befriending Richard Savage, but it was often very helpful. Like a nagging father, Man had cautioned Fielding not to let the opportunity come to nothing: 'There's certainly a better future for you, Henry, in Drury Lane than in Little Turnstile.' And the former thief-catcher had been quick to agree.

Yet now he was gone – at latest report, even now registering himself in the faculty of letters at the University of Leyden. An unexpected, unthinking move: none of his friends could account for it. But the watchman remembered where he had sent the package entrusted to him by the enduring grandmother of Sophia Sinclair. And he remembered, too, what it was to be twenty years old and full of visions.

In the brilliance of Queen Street, Man was suddenly gladdened by the shimmering coat of a standing horse. The sight made him walk even faster, more eagerly. He was on his way to pick up Sarah, to bring her home again.

True, the circumstances could not make him happy, yet he did not feel sad. Sarah's mother, Hester Wells, had died in her sleep yesterday evening, aged seventy-one years. The parish officer had recorded her death on the last day of the legal year, 24 March, 1728, but to her family she had been gone for weeks. Man had loved her, and he could feel the loss; but he had no sorrow for her dying. He had met Charlotte Sinclair.

The house in Dartmouth Street wore the sun as brightly as ever. And in the front hallway Man was welcomed by the highly polished surfaces, the comforting neatness, the smell of a close and living warmth. The mistress of the house was still here.

The signpainter, Michael Wells, was standing in the hall with his only daughter. He gave Man a peaceful smile from a face worn with time, but still undamaged and strong – no different from the examples of his work that the watchman had seen swaying over countless streets.

Sarah was taking leave of her father.

'Now you're to call for me whenever I'm needed. I'll never be too far off, you know. With Daniel still away, who can say how often you'll be wanting someone to bring you your brandy or your pipe or your favourite book? I'm your family now, Father, and I won't leave you to live your days and nights all alone.' She kept drifting back away from the front door. 'Maybe if I were to stay by you but one day more—'

The signpainter reached forward to take his daughter in his arms, kiss her cheek, stroke her hair with his hard hand. Then he let her go.

'Now the door's behind you there, girl. And here's one come to take you to your own street.'

The Mans did not talk much on their way back to Ironmonger Row. The waking season, the lively city, and being together again were enough for them. Instinctively as they walked along, the sides of their arms brushed against each other, intimate and comforting.

Somewhere in Aldersgate Street, Sarah asked her husband about the ailing Formosan, George Psalmanaazaar.

'He is failing fast, I'm afraid. But any man who daily doses himself according to Sydenham's preparation with twelve or so drops of opium cannot surely ask for better.'

Sarah clicked her tongue in sympathy.

'Perhaps a moral book would enliven him some. What do you think, George? We still have Mr Law's *Serious Call*, don't we? I could carry it over to him this evening.'

It was at this point that the watchman stumbled – but it could have been the uneven road.

'No, Sarah, no. Ah – you have so much to do tonight at home. I'll take it myself, will that serve?'

Sarah Man had her face turned towards the other side so her husband could not see her teasing smile.

'You know best, George. You know best.'

The Brothers of Glastonbury

Kate Sedley

August, 1476: Roger the travelling chapman – whose sharp wit and tender heart have been involved in affairs touching the mightiest and humblest in the land – ought to be on his way home to Bristol after a peaceful summer's peddling. But a request from the Duke of Clarence to escort a young bride travelling to meet her betrothed takes him instead to Wells – and an extraordinary adventure. For the bridegroom has vanished, and his brother soon follows.

Roger links the disappearances to the discovery of an ancient manuscript written in a strange language. But as he gradually deciphers the manuscript's meaning, he concludes that a greater mystery still may lie at the heart of the brothers' disappearance . . .

'Weaves a compelling puzzle into the vividly coloured tapestry of medieval life' *Publishers Weekly*

'An attractive hero and effective scene-setting' *Liverpool Daily Post*

0 7472 5877 5

HEADLINE

Jane and the
Unpleasantness at
Scargrave Manor

Stephanie Barron

To Jane Austen's surprise, her visit to the estate of young and beautiful Isobel Payne, Countess of Scargrave, is far from dull. She has scarcely arrived when the Earl is felled by a mysterious and agonizing ailment. His death seems a cruel blow of fate for the newly married Isobel. Yet the widow soon finds that it's only the beginning of her misfortune . . . as she receives a sinister missive accusing her and the Earl's nephew of adultery – and murder.

Afraid that the letter will expose her to the worst sort of scandal, Isobel begs her friend Jane for help. Which is how Jane finds herself embroiled in an investigation that will have her questioning the motives of Scargrave Manor's guests, stumbling upon the scene of a bloody murder, and following a trail of clues that leads all the way to Newgate Prison and the House of Lords.

'Succeeds on all levels. A robust tale of manners and mayhem that faithfully reproduces the Austen Style – and engrosses to the finish' *Kirkus Reviews*

0 7472 5375 7

HEADLINE

*If you enjoyed this book here is a selection of
other bestselling titles from Headline*